Advance Reviews

"In *shanghai.shanghai.shanghai*, the protagonist Ge writes a story titled 'Cultural Exchange' in which he observes *Bad memory, this is not China today*. Indeed, it is China today that is on Alex Kuo's mind in his brilliant and defiant new novel. Kuo has created a challenging form, the metafictional history-novel-memoir, or MFHNM², a masterpiece of irony, the *trompe d'oeil*, a book supposedly 'translated' by the author. In elastic time, history is the page turner, alongside Ge's quirkily profound observations on music, Chinese cuisine, literature and even fashion. An eternal bridge game is the resolution. The city of Shanghai encapsulates the heartbreakingly muddled history of modern China that dominates the political landscape of the 21st century."

—XU XI, editor and writer, *Habit of a Foreign Sky*, *Hong Kong Rose*

"Mr. Rushdie, Mr. Murakami, let me introduce you to Alex Kuo whose novel *shanghai.shanghai.shanghai* moves effortlessly between China in 1939, 1989, and now. The narrator, Ge, talks to his characters and people from the past as the author crafts a course between fiction and non-fiction to find the truth about China's (and America's) modern histories. There is Lu Xun anger here at history's follies, but also unsparing satire and outrageous humor. A dazzling read, a must for Sinophiles and anyone interested in how we get our truths about China yesterday and today. After eleven previous books, this is Kuo's masterpiece, as innovative and intelligent as any writing you can find."

—ROBERT H. ABEL, painter and writer, *Riding a Tiger*, *The Progress of a Fire*

"Bouncing between 1939, 1989 and 2010 in Shanghai, Alex Kuo wisely and mischievously weaves the crazy inconsistencies, tragedies and coincidences of globalization into a dazzling narrative that thrills, enlightens, and humanizes us. One of our most gifted and audacious storytellers, who fuses Gone with the Wind, American missionaries in China, and the 2008 Beijing Olympics to both celebrate and expose the cultural mishaps and hypocrisies of our modern world."

—AIMEE PHAN, columnist and writer, *The Reeducation of Cherry Truong*,
We Should Never Meet

"An inimitable blend of fiction, cultural satire and political romance. Imagine taking a stroll through the streets of modern day Shanghai while wearing a monocle that transmits images from a historical Shanghai, where the international settlement held on to the last gasp of its 100-year history. Kuo's most self-assured manifesto of creative autonomy to date, this book takes you around Shanghai and the Chinese mind as no other tour guide could. It's a book that I'll turn to again."

—WEN JIN, Shanghai scholar and critic, *Pluralist Universalism*

"Alex Kuo's *shanghai.shanghai.shanghai* is a tour de force that moves seamlessly through time and space, revealing different layers of the palimpsest that is the grand metropolis of Shanghai—all told from the point of view of a journalist named Ge, who lives and writes simultaneously in present day freewheeling Shanghai and in the city during its wartime occupation by Japan. Kuo's novel is a poet's fever dream and stream of consciousness rumination on the eponymous city, East and West, colonialism, Hollywood, June 4th, the corruption of the nationalist government, and the vicissitudes of life in China today—in all their multivalent complexity and absurdity."

—ANDREA LINGENFELTER, poet and translator, *Candy*,
Farewell My Concubine

"At a time when most of us are racing to reduce our world to facile, 140-character tweets, Alex Kuo has succeeded once again in doing the opposite: creating a novel that celebrates complexity and challenges our most cherished assumptions about culture, history, politics and even writing itself. *shanghai.shanghai.shanghai* is not easy reading, but it is also difficult to put aside, a book filled with passages and personages that play over and over in the mind long after the final page."

—PAULINE CHEN, medical columnist and writer,
Final Exam: A Surgeon's Reflections on Mortality

shanghai.shanghai.shanghai

shanghai.shanghai.shanghai

ALEX KUO

Translated by the author 郭亞力

redbat books

redbat books
2015

Printed in the United States of America

ISBN 978-0-9895924-5-1
Library of Congress Control Number: 2015947835

First Trade Paperback (*Ge*) Edition: November 1, 2015

FURTHER EDITIONS

This work of fiction is presented in four editions,
multiple designs for the key characters traveling in a Möbius continuum.

ORIGINAL:	LIMITED:	LIMITED:	LIMITED:
The Ge Edition	*The Yali Edition*	*The Páshŏu Edition*	*The Kuifang Edition*
Text set in	Text set in	Text set in	Text set in
BLACK	BLACK	REDBAT RED	SEPIA
ORANGE		BLACK	BLACK
CYAN	Photos in		
PLUM	GREYSCALE	Photos in	Photos in
RED		GREYSCALE	GREYSCALE
GREEN	ISBN		
SEPIA	978-0-9895924-7-5	ISBN	ISBN
		978-0-9895924-8-2	978-0-9895924-9-9
Photos in			
COLOR			
GREYSCALE			
ISBN			
978-0-9895924-5-1			

Published by
redbat books
2901 Gekeler Lane
La Grande, OR 97850
www.redbatbooks.com

Text set in multiple English and Chinese typefaces. A key has been placed on page 217.

Book design by Kristin Summers, redbat design | www.redbatdesign.com

ALSO BY ALEX KUO

This is a novel I imagine I would have written had I been born in Shanghai instead of Boston. As it is, none of it happened, but all of it is true nevertheless, perhaps even more so. Such is the generosity of fiction, and the impudence of the stories we tell, on either side of the Pacific. We both take our days one at a time, on whichever side of the International Date Line, or whether they occurred in the past, future, or present, in whatever order and in whatever tense, same damn thing.

If the truth be told, this imagined author wrote this novel, at least most of it: I only provided some unsolicited assistance here and there—suggested using different type faces for the five narrative voices, formatted some references, abbreviated Tiananmen Square and triple Shanghai with superscript, altered the tense in a couple of episodes, pasted in several backstory sidebars, stretched a few short sentences, tucked in an occasional long paragraph, and let him use my printer when his ran out of ink—though he didn't ask for them or need them, before or after my translation. Hopefully in the end it all came out just right, same time, same place, in Chinese or in English, so to speak.

[Author's note]

PUBLISHER'S NOTE
TO THE READER:
SINCE THIS NOVEL USES
SEVERAL ENGLISH & CHINESE
TYPEFACES TO CLARIFY THE
NARRATIVE VOICES IN THE STORY,
A KEY APPEARS AT THE END
OF THE BOOK ON PAGE 217.

shanghai.shanghai.shanghai

Introduction

This novel begins in 1939, not whenever.

It was a devastating year to most people born in Shanghai or Warsaw early in the century, but a boom year to tinsel town's Selznick International that produced *Gone with the Wind*; today it means almost nothing to most people garrisoned within their social networking platforms.

But this novel also begins in 2010, not whenever.

As the central focus of the 2014 Grand International, a Shanghai artist had located his grandmother's gold fillings and juxtaposed them with all of her leftover wartime household belongings in an installation piece that stretched out over the entire first floor of the metropolitan. *PLEASE DO NOT STEP ON THESE COCKROACHES.* They are part of this exhibition, and reflect his mother's metaphor for those who for whatever reason collaborated with the enemy in the War of Infinite Resistance.

Both the mother and grandmother are long dead, and Warsaw has just unveiled its stunning, paper-folding Polish pavilion in Expo Shanghai. Hollywood has launched its *Flags of Our Fathers'* long-awaited Chinese distribution, and the International exhibition of wartime family memorabilia was only an act of some artist's imagination for a future show, censored no more by the state's official policy than his own cowardice.

Into this scenario comes this novel's central character Ge, the culture writer for the city's promiscuous publication, although he is never entirely sure which Shanghai he is inhabiting, 1939, 2010, or somewhere in between, say the political spring of 1989, that *whenever* necessitating some ambiguous mid-sentence tense shifts for both the author and the reader. Unlike clocks, we do not measure time regularly, but with many different rates of speed and order that coexist, not always rational or coherent, irreconcilable regularities, simultaneous realities.

And there you have it, as simple and convoluted as that, a timepiece that recycles itself in a Möbius warp.

I

Because of the territorial disputes between the movie's distributors and the studio's attorneys negotiating the complicated copyright agreements, it finally got to Shanghai in 2010, four years late. By then most of the audience had already seen it on their underground websites for free, even those illegal films that violate Clause 16 of the Chinese Constitution because they endanger the nation's sovereignty, and territorial integrity, and provoke trouble. But Ge had to review it anyway; for the record, his editor said. Then he took a cab from the newspaper office to Ruijin Cinema on YanAn to catch the early media screening of *Flags of Our Fathers*, for the record, he mimicked and flipped his finger and added to himself in Chinese, Hey, hey, I won't tarnish the national image.

Renyuan or Yuanren, he penciled in the Pitman lined notebook that went with him everywhere—in a pocket during the day or on the table by his bedside that night. The trailers had just ended, the house lights dimmed, and the heavy, purple velvet opened a second time to Metro-Goldwyn-Mayer's golden lion's roar. *It doesn't matter to me what order*

I write it—that's only my pen name anyway. Besides—he wrote this in a note to the editor—*at least twice a week you've printed my byline wrong either way I wrote it, at least since Old Peanut Head left town. That was two years ago exactly, Mr. Editor, when Generalissimo Chiang Kaishek quit the Battle of Shanghai, packed up his troops and sent them upriver to Nanjing to be slaughtered another day,* he added as he flipped over to a new page. *This is 1939 now.*

In addition to writing copy from the Municipal Police desk, he also contributed to the Friday arts and entertainment sections of the English-language newspaper *North China Daily News*. Most of its readers were Chinese and Japanese, then and now, and some British, American, Indian, French, German and Russian too, especially on Fridays. Whether they will stand respectful to the three-minute footage of King George VI at the end of the movie's credits and the limit of his colonial outreach in this British Extraterritorial Settlement west of the Bund in Shanghai will be quite another thing. This patriotic homage will celebrate KGVI in his expedition dress blues as the Emperor of India on horseback reviewing his Coldstream Guards accompanied by *God Save the King* and a fluttering Union Jack, something they weren't required to do at the end of a movie at home in London, and definitely not in Edinburgh, Cardiff or Dublin. *Send him victorious. Happy and glorious.*

Sitting then in the darkened front row of the upstairs lodge section of this cavernous Grand cinema next to the sumptuous Art Deco fronted Sassoon House on the Bund, Ge scribbled down *Gone with the Wind* and copied as many of the opening credits he would need for his review later. *David Selznick* director. *Margaret Mitchell* novel. *Clark Gable, Vivien Leigh*. Distracted by someone who came in late into the front rows, he started abbreviating his notes. *MGM. Stein*. Against the backdrop of the lighted screen, the silhouette was unmistakable: the young, glamorous actress and third wife of the revolutionary Mao Zedong, Jiang Qing, her hair in a trendy blunt cut. Ge could not imagine then that *Gone with the Wind* would become her favorite movie which she would watch at least once a week while she was still in Shanghai and later lip sync in her sleep.

His scribblings on the next page in the notebook were more difficult to decipher, even under the glare of his office's fluorescent lights. But Ge remembered enough to begin the review—if he needed more, he would go to its website. *Actor/director Clint Eastwood has made two movies based on Joe Rosenthal's AP photograph of the U.S. Marines raising their victorious American flag over Iwo Jima's Mount Suribachi and Chicago's Soldier Field during World War II. This iconic image has become the most reproduced picture in the history of photography, culminating in two postage stamps that sold over 200 million licking times.* Instant Pulitzer for all, except for the double American, the Gila River Pima Marine PFC Ira Hamilton Hayes, who was to drown ten years later in two inches of irrigation water.

2

It was close to midnight by the time Ge got back to his desk at the office from the Ruijin. He turned on the lights, made himself a cup of jasmine tea and inserted three sheets of paper into the typewriter's carriage, first making sure the glossy side of the carbon paper between them was facing the platen before rolling them up to line one. Depressed by the movie, he took his time avoiding writing the review.

He started with his byline Renyuan, and using his own calendar, he dated it *15 December, 1939*, and under the title *Raising the Third Flag over Mount Suribachi. The flag of our mothers,* it began. *No one was there with a Speed Graphic at 1/400ᵗʰ of a second on an 8 f-stop to record it. No Pulitzer here. No one to record the broken promises made to our mothers or attempt to mend them.*

He ripped the sheets out of the typewriter, crumpled them and tossed them into the nearest wastebasket. He knew Mr. Editor would have done the same thing. Wrong movie. Wrong date. His fingers were blackened from the cheap carbon paper made way up north in Jilin Province where the Japanese had reenlisted Emperor Puyi as the chief executive of Manchukuo with all of its coal deposits and free lumber. Some of this carbon dust shook loose and landed next to Ge, which he will use to leave traces of himself in the review. He inserted a new set of papers into the Remington and tried to concentrate.

Vivien Leigh… Clark Gable… Hattie McDaniel… in David Selznick's Gone with the Wind *adapted from Margaret Mitchell's novel. The story begins on a large cotton plantation in rural Georgia on the eve of the American Civil War*, he started to write that night, and finished with *Chinese tearjerker romance with Cute Cute Zhang Ziyi in* Crouching Tiger, Hidden Dragon *many years later.* If that's the way you want to waste your tears, he looked at the two women on either side of him glued to the in-flight movie on a Boeing 747 back to Shanghai in 2008. Their eyes were wet, even as they slurped the noodles from their boxed lunch, bits of crackers flaking onto their heaving cleavage, a wet tongue on a nipple, a little kumquat between the legs. Or maybe keep the tears flowing, a couple of times a day, staying in practice for the real thing. But what if there's only a limited supply—then will they have any left for the real thing, or will it escape their recognition? No wonder love stories in Chinese novels, movies, operas and fairy tales always have tragic endings, except for one day a year, on the seventh day of the seventh month.

Either way, Ge decided he would never become a novelist. No chance, not him. No loser him. No chance anyone's going to publish his political novels, not in China, not in the U.S., and maybe not even in the U.K. today, but certainly not now towards the end when Rhett Butler finally said, "Frankly, my dear, I don't give a damn," leaving Scarlett O'Hara sitting on the stairs and weeping in despair. There's no way his fiction's going to compete against these tearjerkers. Oh no, oh no, please make me cry, he mimicked. Trust me; trust me: call me tears.

Ge found out a half century later that what he really wanted to write that night in the newspaper office was an essay on Hong Kong's annual candlelight vigil observing the twenty-fifth anniversary of the 1989 military crackdown on the demonstrations in Beijing's Tiananmen Square. *They won't let go of their hatred for Beijing that goes back at least three generations, like the Miami Cubans for Fidel Castro who booted them out in 1959, or they fled, same thing, or the Chinese who'd swam to Tai-wan in 1949*, he started in his notebook. Or a letter to President Frank-lin D. Roosevelt with a carbon copy to Groucho Marx. *I didn't like the movie; but then I saw it under adverse conditions—in the dark*, which he also saved in English.

3

Ge sorted through his files in the newspaper office and pulled out the photographs he had saved in the last nineteen years for his essay on Tiananmen[2]. First, the AP photo taken of someone identified as Wang Weilin a.k.a. Tank Man on June 5, 1989, by Jeff Widener perched in a sixth floor room of the Beijing Hotel half a mile away with a 400 mm lens on his Nikon FE2. Or one by *Life*'s Stuart Franklin which won him a World Press Award taken at the same time maybe two rooms away on the same floor of the same hotel where foreign correspondents clustered at the rooftop bar at five every afternoon to second source each other's story, lies that loop and come back as corroborating evidence. Or another by *Newsweek*'s Charlie Cole, same date, same time, same place, same subject.

Ge flipped to a page in his worn copy of a 1999 issue of *Time* magazine in which Tank Man had morphed into Unknown Rebel and been designated one of the 100 Most Influential Persons of the 20th century. With a bookbag in one hand and a flag in the other waving a column of People's Liberation Army Norinco Type 59 main battle tanks into submission at T^2, he was designated global human rights hero. We don't need a flag here, not now. Testifying at a House International Relations Human Rights subcommittee meeting in Washington seven years later, Amnesty International's Louisa Coan identified him as a student standing alone in the Avenue of Eternal Peace. Right. Now we have a flag to wave. We have history; we have memory.

PHOTO CREDIT: Jeff Widener of The Associated Press, 1989

Ge looked at these tank photos again. Their gun barrels were plugged—no tank driver was going to be given the option of opening up his 105 mm gun in 'I'^{2} regardless of I.Q., training or experience. No battalion commander was going to take the chance that an errant armor-piercing, high explosive shell might damage Chairman Mao's Mausoleum or his portrait hanging over the entrance to the Gate of Heavenly Peace. Just bring in the tanks for intimidation and crowd control. To show who's the boss, who's in charge here, and fuck the foreign media cameras.

Now, who was that man in front of the tanks who refused to be intimidated and what happened to him? Ge opened another file. A former special assistant to President Richard Nixon reported in 1999 that the masked man was executed fourteen days later. Another file claimed he was shot months later. Still others held out, hopeful he had somehow escaped to Taiwan in

1949, or forty years later flipping his story into a Nieman Fellowship at Harvard University, or just laying low in the Xinjiang Autonomous Region and hiding out with the Uighurs until the right movie script came along.

Then again maybe he was an undercover Public Security Bureau liaison officer to the PLA and marking out the picket line for the tank drivers, and his satchel housed his field radio to HQ? Maybe he was a bored Bank of China accountant who had too much to drink for lunch. Maybe he was just caught up in the moment and, aware that the lights were on and cameras rolling worldwide, acted out the expected role before Steven Spielberg or Mel Gibson or David Wolper or Ken Burns or Henry Louis Gates had a chance to turn it into a universal icon.

Ge could not write any of this in American free-style and not sound Chinese, however appropriate the anger and the fury; and he could not write this in Chinese because no American would ever believe him. But maybe none of this mattered, since he was not writing fiction, remember? He was doing journalism. So Ge thought as he looked at the last picture again, the end. The best part was over, he'd missed it, he had come in too late. But that's all he's got, this one picture. This was the only memory that has been recorded, all the emotions coalesced into this one visual icon, and nothing is going to change any of it, nothing. It has become history, in the same way as *Gone with the Wind*, the memory moving forward and backward in the absolute present.

4

Early into the morning and nearing the print deadline for the movie review, Ge looked at the second set of photographs. Joe Rosenthal had his Speed Graphic with him at Iwo Jima that day for the second flag raising on Mount Suribachi, the one that's staged, the one taken in the afternoon. It became the most reproduced picture in the history of photography and went on to win ten Oscars, including Best Picture. Like the picture of the masked man flagging down the column of PLA tanks in T^2 fifty years later, this too will become history, a history of Georgia plantation life on Tara where the mansion up on the hill with wide lawns and breezy open space kept away the *Anopheles gambiae* and the *Plasmodium vivax* epidemic running amok through Georgia and the other Ku Klux Klan states.

Ge shook his hair and decided for now it's easier to tackle the movie version. The piece on T^2 and *Gone with the Wind's* companion movie *Django Unchained* will just have to wait until the next anniversary, unless the Hong Kong freelance writer PK Leung beats him to it. Too many competing domains and simultaneous realities to sort through right now.

Maybe bring it up with Kuifang at dinner tonight, since he's not sure he wanted to continue their last conversation about getting married, in the past, now, or in the future, or why it mattered at all, or not. She'll have a pragmatic answer for most complications in life.

Wanted to or not, the three surviving members of the second flag-raising Marines including PFC Ira Hayes were air-lifted home out of battle in an Army Air Force C-47 and thrust into a public relations tour to sell war bonds, launched by yet a third flag-raising, staged this time in the heartland for 100,000 spectators in Soldier Field on Lake Shore Drive, now home to the American football team the Chicago Bears, he wrote.

Yeah right, a record of how Hollywood has shaped the American imagination of Asia is more like it, Ge signed to himself, in case anyone was listening as he pedaled his bicycle back to the office to write the review. Imagination all right. It'll become part of America's collective memory since no historian is about to flip it, in no magazine, no newspaper, no book, no village quilt or talk radio, no YouTube or Twitter, no blog or Facebook or Instagram, copyrighted or not, not even for a patented merit badge, in any language or text message; in a couple of generations on this side of the Pacific we're going to start believing this version too, he muttered in Chinese, since everyone under twenty will be slurping from this same global trough, and we'll all end up seeing and believing Asian history as produced and distributed by Hollywood, or the behemoth Hengdian Studios just a short bullet train ride south of Shanghai, same thing.

And just for the record, he typed into his computer—although he knew his editor would vet these next two paragraphs—*in the quarter century between 1942 and 1968, John Wayne alone starred in twelve movies that caricatured and demeaned Asians. Count them:* Back to Bataan, Blood Alley, Donovan's Reef, The Fighting Seabees, Flying Leathernecks, Flying Tigers, The Geisha and the Barbarian, The Green Berets, In Harm's Way, Operation Pacific, The Sands of Iwo Jima, They were Expendable—*Chinese, Japanese, Filipino, Vietnamese, take your pick.*

And for the record, the rodeo cowboy, stuntman and actor Yakima Canutt from Colfax Washington had doubled for both Clark Gable's Rhett Butler and John Wayne in Shanghai as Captain Tom in *Blood Alley,* where his co-star Lauren Bacall as the Protestant missionary daughter Cathy asked him to free her from the yoke of the ChiComs, this supplication repeated to Steve McQueen as Machinist Mate First Class in *The Sand Pebbles* and Clark Gable as Hank Lee in *Soldier of Fortune.*

5

Two years ago in 1937 Generalissimo Chiang Kaishek was a different sort of soldier of fortune than Hank Lee in the movie, when he changed his mind in the middle of the battle and withdrew his best weapons and most experienced units against the stymied Japanese onslaught in Shanghai.

[At this point the author's literary agent asked him to segue into a sidebar for the benefit of the reader unfamiliar with the history of World War II on the other side of the Pacific, other than vaguely aware that to end the war a WMD was dropped on Hiroshima and a second on Naga-saki three days later in 1945. The author consent-ed, after losing his argument that introducing the historian's neutral voice at this point would be the *kiss of death* for his novel in which he is attempting to get at what really happened and why. They eventually agreed and accepted us-ing the buttoned-down Arial Narrow font for this section as a compromise.]

The generalissimo had started the campaign by asking his troops to fight to the last man, beginning with the *Bloody Saturday* debacle in August during which his Italian-trained pilots flew six American Curtis Hawk III biplane sorties that not only failed to reach the Japanese vessels anchored in the Huangpu River just five minutes north of the airstrip, including the flagship, the armored cruiser *Izumo* built in Newcastle, England, but whose stray bombs killed hundreds of Chinese civilians instead.

PHOTO CREDIT: Imperial Japanese Navy

How does one write about war? For that matter, how does one talk about war, or even think about it, when eventually we must face our broken promises and the endless line of women and children who walk from one poor, devastated country to another poor, devastated country?

For historians and popular novelists, that's another matter, whether it's Ernest Gann against the ChiComs in *Soldier of Fortune,* or Margaret Mitchell portraying the American Civil War in *Gone with the Wind.*

Or this beginning of World War II in which Generalissimo Chiang relied heavily on his German adviser General Alexander von Falkenhausen's recommendation to base his strategy on eliminating the enemy in one major decisive battle in Shanghai. The experienced general neglected to tell Chiang about the genesis of this approach, derived from the 18th century Prussian Philipp von Clausewitz's military theories published in his *On War*, when he had never won a battle or war in his entire military career, and had instead been Napoleon's prisoner early in the century. But his post mortem dialectical lies about superior planning, strategy and tactics earned him Hitler's admiration years later when the Führer issued the suicidal orders to his personal staff in the last two weeks of the war in his name, Operation Clausewitz.

After a lunch with Mayling Soong in early October, Old Peanut Head reversed his strategy in a critical moment in the battle and followed his wife's suggestion instead. Madame Chiang had her personal army, all women with cowboy hats, two gassed DC-3s parked nearby for a quick escape, with one navy ensign and two marine pfcs standing by 24/7 to move her Steinway CDs across China, from Shanghai to Hangzhou, Nanjing, Chongqing, Xian, Chengdu, or any point in between, or in any combination just one gastank ahead of the Japanese Imperial Army or Mao Zedong's Red Army with or without the Eighth Route Army, with or without Joseph Stilwell's approval. But she was also a savant about wealth, power and death.

Along with her siblings, she learned at an early age that real power and influence came from the ability to anticipate death and hence to avoid it and exploit that clairvoyance over others. Her husband on the other hand didn't have such *fuqiang*, and needed weekly ablutions from her and the protection of Shanghai's Green Gang. But the Green Gang could not extend its power against the Japanese Imperial Army one hundred and eighty miles west to Nanjing two months later, when an average of fifty thousand civilians were massacred every week for six weeks, almost ten thousand a day.

And Madame Chiang was no help either, her cheerleaders, two Steinway CDs and enough gold bars for the rest of the war plus some, had flown to Chongqing two months earlier in her two DC-3s right after that lunch with her husband.

After the Japanese defeated the generalissimo in November, Shanghai was left warily divided into the French Concession, International Settlement, Chinese City, Little Tokyo and two other subdivisions, with the Municipal Police and several other overlapping and competing authorities keeping order under the watchful eyes of the Japanese and the spymaster Dai Li, at least for the first part of the war, with checkpoints along the ambiguous borders and bridges between the extraterritorial residencies, especially porous if one had American dollars or cigarettes or nylons or Hersheys or Trojans or Similac. The Grand and the Cathay continued to show the most recent Hollywood movies, someone from the British Legation was seen riding along the Bund on a brand new Triumph 5T, and the Shanghai International Bridge Club continued to hold its weekly Wednesday night duplicate game on Mohawk Road.

6

Yes, Shanghai was under the watchful eye of the superspy Dai Li, but one was never quite sure for whom he was really working as he jostled with the military attachés and commerce exchequers from London, Berlin, Washington, Paris, Moscow and Rome at official receptions, theatrical openings, building dedications, or undercover along the congested streets filled with immigrants from everywhere trying to get into the International Settlement with or without papers, with or without gold, with or without food and water, and with his ear to the ground, Ge heard that Dai is the only one on the planet who did not have to park his pistol when he came into Dodge or Old Peanut Head's bedroom day or night, a trust unheard of in Chinese history, not since the 18th century publication of its first classic, ha ha, the novel unreadable in Chinese or English—and Ge has tried many times, really—Cao Xueqin's *The Dream of the Red Chamber* that explored betrayal, family malfeasance, gambling, revenge, assassination, motifs since imbedded into its national DNA, and the flimsy difference between collaboration and corroboration that usually accompanied dynastic or regime change. In this way Ge became intrigued with writing an imaginary interview with Dai, planning to run it by the competing *Shanghai Evening and Mercury* if his own paper optioned the first refusal, *because*, Mr. Editor will say again, *a newspaper is a newspaper, it doesn't publish fiction, no matter how true it is.* For now it'll just have to wait, as he followed Kuifang into a curtained booth on the second floor of her fourth successful Xi'an restaurant in Shanghai, the Tang and Qin on the broad RuiHong Lu.

Over an appetizer of balsamic pear and red jujube with honey, Ge asked if she'd a good day.

No, she said and tugged on her chartreuse pique jacket, her Mandarin almost perfect even though she's been in Shanghai from the far northwest Shaanxi Province for less than seven years.

What happened?

Why share bad days; one is enough not to repeat it in the telling, *ma*? She smiled at him and leaned her head to one side to show her tart retro short bob, with a Veronica Lake's peek-a-boo to the side.

Why can't we talk like normal people, Ge asked and sipped on his apricot tea.

Ge, that's not a thought. Just noise. There's too much of it in people already.

You're right. You're right of course. Like you said you won't marry me last time because you're never quite sure when you'll see me next, tomorrow morning maybe, or maybe fifty years from now, right, you said?

In her white silk blouse with the elaborate sleeves, Kuifang reached behind her and brought out a copy of this month's issue of the urban modernist review *Gudao*. A present for you, she said, from the newsstand down the street, here in 1939, and arguing like a married couple who's been married for more than seven years *ma*?

And you might want to write something for them, this year, she added with emphasis.

You mean it got past the security surveillance of the Bureau of Investigation and Statistics and the Japanese too? They have eyes and ears everywhere.

Now it's called the State Administration of Press, Publication, Radio, Film and Television, and it definitely is not going to allow anyone to make a bungee jump from the top of the Bank of China Tower, especially at night, and most especially not some resistance stories by young women writers they believe out of ideological control, Kuifang said with some urgency. And do it now, before everyone disappears.

With dusk approaching, they both looked across the river at the lights coming on the triple towers in a row, the Jin Mao, the Oriental Pearl and the Bank of China Tower where Kuifang has her bridge game on the 52nd floor, and on a dry and clear evening like this one, they were captured by ten thousand tourist digital images.

Make that fifty thousand, Ge corrected himself, these towers[3] that have appeared on the expensive east side of the river almost overnight in the short six years since his graduation from Fudan.

7

In preparation for his imaginary interview with Dai Li, Ge spent hours gathering background information in the library and from the Internet, finding Doctor Google particularly unreliable, even when he was able to access it through *Google Hong Kong*.

After two weeks, he found the work of Milton Miles, Oliver Caldwell, and Shen Zui most compelling in the complicated, competing and overlapping espionage networks lurking in the shadows of occupied Shanghai in 1939.

> Milton Miles was the far eastern chief of the American Office of Strategic Services (OSS), which in 1947 morphed into the Central Intelligence Agency (CIA). Recent documents have revealed a surprising array of American agents who had worked in China during World War II as OSS operatives, including Julia Child.

A graduate of the Annapolis Naval Academy and retired a rear admiral, Miles admired Dai Li and approved a request for a large order of Smith and Wesson revolvers, Colt 45s, and Thompson submachine guns for Dai's not-so-secret agency. Born in China of American Methodist missionaries, Oliver Caldwell returned during the war as an American Army captain and worked as an analyst for the OSS. In his book published by Southern Illinois University Press some quarter of a century after the end of the war, he described the corruption and dysfunction of Generalissimo Chiang's government, and suspected that everyone in his security apparatus was either a Japanese or Green Gang mole or double agent. Shen Zui was once Dai Li's deputy chief heavily involved in the gun-and-knife death squads and torturous vetting of double agents and moles. In the early 1930s, he nicknamed Dai the Monkey King, a trickster who could cheat death. Dismayed with Dai's establishment of one secret alliance after another, Shen started to turn against him, convinced that he was a despotic tyrant—a *baojun zhuanzhi zhuyi*—running a fascist secret service.

Ge could grasp the idea of a secret society such as the armed Society for Common Progress headquartered in the French Concession, as if China needed another secret society, but he had trouble with secret alliances and how these two words seem to contradict each other in meaning, until Kuifang reminded him that *Dream of the Red Chamber* relied heavily on such amorphous relationships which because of their secrecy could change from week to week. Even so, they both remained on his list of prepared questions to ask Dai as he entered his dark office.

At first Ge did not see him sitting in the shadows on a wooden chair to the side of a small desk until his clear, pleasant voice invited him to sit in the only other chair in the room, the one behind the desk's drawers.

Qǐng zuò.

Ge was already making mental notes: short, like the Monkey King, wide-eyed, face of a very important person, a snorting horse, *mǎ*, the most powerful man in all China, a single light-bulb in a movie studio set of a black op interrogation site duplicated in a hundred movies.

When he looked up from his notes, the basement room's fluorescent lights came on and Dai had emerged from the shadows, an imposing man with an erect back.

You the reporter from the morning English newspaper?

Yes.

Then get on with it. Use your notes if you have to. I know you are prepared.

Ge glanced down at his list of questions.

Q-1. Is it true you changed your name from childhood to *Li* to rub out your past, reflecting the clandestine nature of your career?

Q-2. Are you working on military or political intelligence, or do you think they are the same?

Q-3. How far have you penetrated the German and Japanese intelligence networks and what are they doing with each other?

Q-4. How can you work for both the OSS and Chiang Kaishek's secret service when they seem to be subverting each other with double agents, moles, and sometimes triple agents, whatever they are?

Q-5. Do you know Julia Child?

Q-6. The name of the Investigation and Statistics Bureau is so harmless sounding, especially its nickname, Number 76. What does it really do?

Q-7. Why are there so many secret societies and secret alliances in Shanghai? In China? In life?

```
Q-8.   Is it true that you have a dozen concentration
       camps chock full of tortured, emaciated men and
       women arrested because they were union workers or
       communist sympathizers?
Q-9.   Are you a collaborator or a corroborator?
Q-10.  Who do you really work for?
```

By the time Ge got to the end of the list, the lights had dimmed and he found himself in an empty room, tethered to a notebook with more questions beyond the sleep of his neighbors that will keep him awake for years.

8

Our author has hacked into the Word files in Ge's *MacBook Pro* and downloaded a copy of his imaginary interview with Dai Li under the title of "The True Story of Ah Zee."

For several years now I have been meaning to write the true story of Ah Zee, it began in the first person. I did not want to use metaphors or irony because they can come back and bite you, it continued in this detached voice of a reporter, except for a few intrusions into the narrative where Ge got bored. It took me years, but finally I decided I didn't want to make up anything; it'll be best if there were no lies in this story, since they take on a life of their own and all too often end up exacting fatal costs from those who buy into these concocted realities. So, like Dante and Joyce, the names and dates in this story will all be real, and the consequential harm to those guilty ones is therefore intentional. Except that here and there, there'll be some invented detail and other weapons to make the story more readable and come out right and strike home.

Ah Zee had always wanted to be a writer. After his in-consequential middle school education in which he silently suspected his teachers were Confucian imbeciles, he left his isolated village against his parents' wishes and worked his way downriver to the coast. He had read that Shanghai was the mecca for writers and anyone who wanted to be a writer had to live and work there, soak up the urban, modern life, and make career connections.

At first he got by as a kitchen slave in a restaurant in the International Settlement, washing dishes and taking out the garbage, but his dedication and manners caught the atten-tion of the owner who placed him first as a bus boy in the downstairs dining room, then within a year promoted him to be a uniformed doorman, bowing and greeting all the cus-tomers with his wide smile and good looking teeth. The own-er was so impressed with Ah Zee's consistency in meeting the guests' needs that within another year he only had to work the day shift, leaving his evenings and weekends free to pur-sue the life of a writer.

Ever attentive to the conversations of the guests and from reading newspapers and reviews in the public library, he knew the names and reputations of several Shanghai literary societies, including the Crescent Moon, the conservative Mandarin Duck, Butterfly and Hippopotamus, and its ideological opposite, the Shanghai League of Left-Wing Writers. He learned that some of them met weekly in the same district where he worked. Once he thought he saw Lu Xun enter the bistro across the street.

One evening he managed to introduce himself as a novice writer to the stylish woman with hair in a bobbed, tidy, blunt cut who frequented the restaurant by herself and belonged to one of these societies, and managed to solicit an invitation to come to its next weekly discussion group meeting where she would introduce him to other writers with similar interests.

Within a month his networking expanded, and although he had not been asked to join any of these societies, he would attend their meetings at least twice a week, and quickly memorized the names of these philosophers, publishers, editors and writers who drank and talked all night, especially those who drank and talked the most. They would fire endless abstract lectures at each other—sometimes standing and gesturing with a wine bottle for emphasis—about the nature and function of art, the difference between fiction and non-fiction, the Quacks always taking the draconian position of resisting all changes in form or content, and the League members ready to join the labor unions, pass out leaflets, man the barricade and paint public murals. Sometimes a writer would read an early draft of a short story as if he's in a writers' workshop, usually followed by a polite, pattering of hands and a short, supportive discussion.

Once in a while Ah Zee would participate and say something very slowly and deliberately, but no one could ever remember what he had said, since he would always carefully rephrase in different words what someone had already said ten minutes ago, and his critique of the story-in-progress so full of hollow praises that even the author could not recall what Ah Zee had said a minute later. Careful not to draw any attention to himself, he soon became invisible.

But he was determined to change all that. He was going to write an original story, and then they would look up to him and recognize him for what he was. He had been thinking about this for several weeks, even when he was greeting the lunch guests at the restaurant. He was determined to make himself visible by writing.

Ah Zee finally settled on writing a story based on an imaginary interview with the financier T.V. of the powerful Soong family, the tycoon who bankrolled Generalissimo Chiang Kaishek's political adventures, and on several occasions provided the ransom money when he or one of his political or criminal friends could not find safe passage with the warlords. Because wealth and power were coalesced into one word in their mother tongue, *fuqiang*, T.V. Soong was probably the most important man in Chiang's government at the beginning of World War II, in much the same way that Dai Li was the most dangerous, at least the most feared.

(800)

> At this point our author noticed a double-spaced break in the narrative preceded by a parenthetical numeric eight hundred, as if Ge were expecting this imaginary interview would be published serially.

He knew that in order to get his story past the security scrutiny of the Bureau of Investigation and Statistics (BI&S), he would have to make sure its final draft would be non-threatening to China's national identity, the next installment began after the break. It would have been a lot easier had he written poetry, as the censors and analysts didn't even bother to look at poetry because they knew that no one reads poetry and no one understands it, including the poet. But it definitely would not be acceptable for any writer to portray the nation's leaders as talking in nasal duck voices and dressed up in bad fitting off-the-rack western suits looking like cadavers with hair pieces designed by morticians, having just attended a leadership workshop in which they learned how to project facile, neutral facial expressions and to place their hands over their crotch with toes pointed slightly out, the benevolent leaders with thick, black plastic eyeglass frames, exposed for all media cameras, domestic and international. Above all, they would never smile, only grin when they had to, slightly, as if it were a mistake.

Ah Zee was not going to make a mistake here, not at this point of his budding writing career. In preparation for putting a scrubbed and sanitized appearance to the story, he would begin by putting together a list of ten soft questions and emailing them to T.V. Soong's communicators for advance vetting. These neutered questions would be positioned a little to the left of Chiang and a little to the right of Mao Zedong, about dead middle politically, where it would be impossible for anyone to remember what was said and what he looked like. In other words, he thought it'll be a clever approach to prompt the readers to discover within themselves the answers they already knew. It'll make them proud, real proud, and ready to go out to campaign and vote because they'd become smart from reading a newspaper.

Q-1.   Is it true your father Charlie Soong went to America's Duke University and came back to China a Methodist missionary printing and selling the Bible in Shanghai that made him a very rich man?

ALEX KUO

Q-2. Is it true you yourself went to America's Harvard University?

Q-3. You have three sisters. Is it true one of them married the richest man in China, H.H. Kung? Another, the father of China's struggle for independence, Dr. Sun Yatsen? And the third, the Generalissimo Chiang Kaishek?

Q-4. Did you initiate steps to curry Russia's favor and lower its import tariffs on Chinese merchandise by drawing up a proposal to award Vladimir Putin the Confucius Peace Prize, for bringing safety and stability to Russia?

Q-5. Was it difficult moving the entire government from Nanjing to Chongqing?

Q-6. What about moving all the heavy industrial equipment to the interior from the coastal areas and away from the Japanese bombs?

Q-7. Do you know Julia Child?

Q-8. Has your friendship with the American media tycoon Henry Luce made it easier to solicit the support of the American public for the Nationalist government?

Q-9. As you know, Henry Luce's parents were American missionaries in China, as were Pearl Buck's. Have you read her novel *The Good Earth*, and what did you think of it?

Q-10. And finally, what are you going to do when this war is over?

As a further precaution against the BI&S, Ah Zee decided to submit his story to a newspaper seven hundred and fifty miles to the north, the *Beijing Morning News*, so that he would not be recognized as its author, for much the same reason he had changed his name years ago to the last letter of the Roman alphabet, *Z*, so that he would be the last person to be remembered and accused of something, anything at all.

Within an hour of the Web publication of this imaginary interview and T.V. Soong's answers that provided nothing the public had not already known for decades, Shanghai's literary societies were humming with network chatter. The story's middle position disturbed those on the political left and the political right, and because it said nothing, nothing at all, it did not take them long to point their collective fingers at the person they could not remember: Ah Zee.

At the meeting of the conservative Hippopotamus group the following week, a meeting that included members from the League of Left-Wing Writers, Ah Zee had to face a tribunal of writers, mural artists and union organizers. They took turns yelling at him. Some said he was better suited to write corporate press kits. One thought voters who based their votes on reading the newspaper should have their right to vote taken away. Another suggested giving Ah Zee an appointment in the Bureau of Self-Censorship.

By the time it was midnight, all the wine gone and ideological positions exhumed and exhausted, Ah Zee suggested a compromise: he will submit a retraction and personally courier it to the editorial offices in Beijing on the next bullet train.

As the meeting was breaking up, someone heard Lu Xun say, "China is now being ruled by such people like Ah Zee."

(1,600)

9

Tired from holding up the double mirrors to look into that endless story-within-the-story-within-the-story, Ge walked into the washroom, leaned both hands on a basin counter, and under the fluorescent light looking into yet another mirror, he saw someone who looked exactly like him in reverse looking back at him, in the same black t-shirt and black jeans, wondering if they were writing the same story, and if anyone out there understood what they wrote, or even cared. Who do you think you are, he asked, and who do you think you are writing to? You're the culture critic, re-voicing, impersonating, reorganizing, always pillaging someone else's life. People like you are shoplifters and should always be under the careful eye of the spymaster.

Ge tried to see Ah Zee in the mirror, if he was average looking, medium height, medium build, pants slightly darker than his shirt, eyes no one can remember in the shadow of a head that was not round, square, or pointed or looking at you. He wanted to talk to him, he wanted to find out what it was like being in the middle of everything.

But it came out as Are you a thief disguised as a writer, his question resonating in the basin below him.

There you are, a familiar voice answered behind him. Are you talking to yourself again?

Looks like you have something for me, an assignment, no? Ge asked his editor's reflection in the mirror, a two-dimensional digital image easier to face than its original behind him.

Yes. Mr. Editor placed a G-train ticket on the washroom counter. Do a piece on the 798 Art Zone. It's been around for more than ten years. About time we did something. A weekend magazine cover feature.

Why, Ge protested, his usual first reaction to a new assignment that he didn't like. Why? It's dead. Its only real life was its first five years. Now it's been turned into a zone of bistros and designer chopsticks and high-end clothes and overpriced fusion art by professor-type artists from the Academy and Tsinghua, just like the American Santa Fe. Great place for partying and a great post-industrial chic location for a Christian Dior perfume launch.

Are you done?

No, not yet. It's over, gentrified, went from avant-garde to BoBo in less than the blink of one eye. Ullens has already made its fortune ripping off contemporary Chinese art and is closing at the end of the year. The only important and good art left are Wu Didi's six new pieces at the Shone Shaw Gallery. Besides that, her home gallery is right here at Shine Art Space, just down the street, he pointed into the mirror.

You already got your way when we pulled you away from the police blotter. Now you want to make your own assignments? You know Ge, you're an arrogant little shit.

Yeah? So? Ge asked, finally turning around to face his editor. The only reason you keep me around's that you know there isn't anyone alive in Shanghai who can write better. And as long as we're into this contract renegotiation talk without any representative from HR, that means all of China, for all that matters.

That's enough of this. Straight writing, mind you, in the third person, and not one of your critical missiles. And in my computer by Wednesday morning.

After his editor left, Ge looked back into the mirror for a long time and thought about starting to smoke again, before picking up the bullet train ticket and leaving for the Hongqiao station on the other side of the river.

Life keeps on lasting as long as I keep on writing, a way of bending corners.

ALEX KUO

10

Tired and stiff after a drawn out twenty-six hour train ride with two engine changes at Nanjing and Jinan, Ge walked out of the Beijing Station. Under the dim streetlights in an unusual clear night, he took a deep breath of cool air away from the puff-and-hiss of the steam engines, and decided to walk instead. Into this urban quiet then and past the late spring blush of rose and peony in hedge and wall, clutching his duffel, he wound his way west through the maze of the U-district alleyways until he found the hotel by Vega, his closest starlight west over Haidian.

I'll begin with a list of celebrities who've come to 798 in the last two years, Ge started writing his piece over a morning coffee and croissant at the Starbucks around the corner. Cindy Crawford, Sir Elton John, both Zhang Liji and Amy Tan even though they seem to be writing the same damn story, and Jodie Foster, the Art Zone's first celebrity contact. He doesn't want me to use *BoBo* in the article, but I'll shuffle *bohemian* and *bourgeoisie* and insert them into the image captions. First I need to jump the government's wall and download a VPN to speed up my Internet searches—when I was digging for backstory material for the Dai Li piece, it took forever to upload and operate the Google search engine. Kuifang's mentioned *PandaPow* has worked best for finding fresh local produce for her kitchens, and it's free.

After headlining 798 ArtZone for the weekend magazine feature, Ge described a short history of how the Germans and Russians fought over its architectural design before breaking ground in 1954, opening a factory for industrial sound systems, both civilian and military. The Russians wanted an ornamental design with cheaper materials, but the Germans won with its concept that fused function with form, a design principle left over from their Bauhaus contribution to modernism, and the use of better materials. When it was completed three years later, it became one of the most productive factories in China, and survived to be the only positive feature of Chairman Mao's murderous Great Leap Forward that resulted in more than forty-five million deaths. Ge was certain Mr. Editor will delete this last line on his computer, as well as the next one that claimed Germany's two positive contributions to Chinese culture were its design of this factory and the Qingdao brewery out on the coast, followed by the observation that the Germans did not let a colonizing moment slip by when they established a resident orchestra which played excerpted popular 19th century German romantic classics in free concerts on Sunday afternoons, especially Richard Wagner's *Ride of the Valkyries.*

With the emergence of new technological demands, the factory became obsolete and was shut down forty years later. The spacious buildings with the high ceilings attracted Beijing's Central Academy of Fine Arts' administrators, and in 1995 several faculty artists moved their studios to this site, followed by other artists, writers, musicians, fashion designers and school drop outs, accompanied by galleries, bistros, boutiques, bars and tea houses, a definite challenge to Shanghai's lead on fashionista, cultural innovation and production.

Within a few short years, entrepreneurial foreigners with no apparent ideological agenda swooped in and exhausted the market potential of modern Chinese art, and quickly gentrified the area into a tourist destination attraction. They included the Belgian Baron Guy Ullens de Schooten, as well as Americans such as the Texans Robert Berndell who could turn on or off his Texas Ranger accent in his Timezone 8 Art Books, and the middle sibling Neil between 19th century opium-running, Yankee-Clipper-Trader descendants Jeb and George Bush, who started buying up all the golf courses and shooting galleries in Beijing.

After ending his piece with an admiring and illustrated look at Wu Didi's six new abstract oil paintings of insects and tiny, geologic objects, Ge emailed it to his editor in Shanghai, before taking a cab to the South Station for his return trip to Shanghai. Straight up. Third person. Riveting illustrations. And only three toxic indulgences for Mr. Editor to delete. *Yours, Renyuan.*

II

Ge got back to Shanghai's Hongqiao station in time for lunch on the same morning he had his Starbucks coffee in Beijing. There were two trains here, but Ge will only remember the electric, magnetic bullet G-train that brought him back from Beijing in less than six hours with four stops. At that time he did not know about the other train that's seventy years behind schedule, but he will know about it at some point in the past perfect tense of the author's native language.

At the present moment in 2010, Kuifang and he were talking again about getting married. Did they first meet only a month ago, but were actually married back in 1939? If that's so, then talking about getting married again seventy years later would make sense. The hard part would be to explain what happened in the stretch in between.

For now, Ge's having a quick lunch at her third Xi'an restaurant—the Tang Yun at 300 LongHui Lu on the same side of the river as the train station, the one favored by many Taiwanese businessmen—before going back to the newspaper office. Here Kuifang's eyes were stern and resolute, warning everyone away from voicing any objection they might have against what she was thinking and saying, her staff attentive to all her instructions, even when whispered from a distance, as if they could lip read. She wore the same look last week when she explained in a moment of impatience while brushing her teeth, that she didn't want to get married because she didn't want to look into the same mirror with him in the mornings.

For now she's disturbed by these Han men and their notorious and disturbing reputations flirting with the waitresses at her restaurant. They come with money, and they are here to make more money. There are more than 400,000 of them in Shanghai alone, with more in Vietnam, Thailand, Myanmar, Malaysia and Indonesia. Their Mandarin is terrible, a heavy, cacophonic Shanghai accent as if they had been forced to memorize it from their Shanghai grandparents who had swam across the Black Ditch (Taiwan Strait) to Taiwan in 1949, as if these grandchildren have returned sixty years later in 747s and alien to the language, customs, diet and dress. One can tell who they are by their Rolexes, Prada shoes and the footprints they leave behind. Many of them live in expensive condos, sometimes in Jingtian Lake's gated neighborhoods developed for them. They are mostly men who own their businesses with fluid capital, and their Taiwan dollar goes ten times further here.

In their forties and fifties, most of them are tired of their families and leave them behind in Taipei and take monthly commutes. When they are in Shanghai they become mean and exploitive of women. They recruit and hire local, conducting weeklong casting interviews for innocent, delicious young women just out of college, usually from a rural background and virgins. They pay them to do nothing, fuck them, then terminate the interview by shoving a wad of American Hamiltons into their cleavages with "Scram, time's up," before putting them in a cab for another destination, telling them they are not suited for this job or this town. These victims leave corrected, their love story crushed, but it won't be the first time, before they return home after it's too late.

In the meantime these men continue their festive luncheons and drink, belch and fart too much, much like their Mainland counterpart, except they were writing off their meals on their business accounts while the locals were dining out on the government's renminbi. Kuifang became more disturbed each time they came in, *jiūjié*, worried, feeling un-easy, not sure what to do, sorry, but there is no one word equivalent in English for translating this slang expression. She wanted to protect her staff, especially these young women, including relatives of friends who had come some nine hundred miles from Xi'an to work in one of her restaurants and live in Shanghai for a year or two while deciding what they wanted to do in life. She wasn't about to call security to usher out these clients, as long as they were quiet and obsequiously polite, which they continue to be, for now. She decided she will have a talk with her staff tonight about survival and resistance, in the meantime keeping a threatening eye on the Taiwanese.

12

It is the obsequious look of that undercover Chinese agent sitting at the corner table in this fashionable bistro with his Mauser bulging under his wool tunic that is threatening. In this Japanese-occupied International Settlement where the non-Chinese three percent of the residents were keeping an eye on each other, he could be a double or triple agent, for all anyone knew, including him. He could be working for Dai Li's Number 76, the German *Abwehr*, the Japanese *tokumu kikan*, the American OSS, the British MI6, himself, or all of them, especially the French *Deuxième* Bureau.

Around the corner from this bistro in the shadows of this extraterritorial enclave live a million Chinese ambiguously protected by the porous sovereignty boundaries. Here it's the women who shoulder the consequences of the men's acts of wanton and devastating violence, and their lives and the lives of their children will be forever changed because of it, if they live that long. At least here in Shanghai they're better off than what they knew happened to their sisters in Nanjing two winters ago.

During a break at the back of the bistro, Kuifang was joking around with the three vulnerable young women from Xi'an who have come to Shanghai for work.

Why do we only see one side of the moon, she asked.

Because we are poets, one answered and giggled, and after a thoughtful moment the only one of the three with short hair said, because we are revolutionaries.

We only see the need for a revolution, she explained, and we never think of its other side, the necessary destruction.

Well, Kuifang thought to herself, she won't need any help from me. She'll knock these suckers flat on their butts and volunteer to go north with the Young Reinforcements League in its fight against the Japanese occupation, the only resistance since the other nationalist factions were occupied in killing each other.

Astonished but not surprised, her two friends looked at her and nodded.

Kuifang knew she'd find these two a year later among those left behind foraging for dropped millet husks or cueing up in thick lines for hours with their empty wash basins and kitchen pots for drinking water and if lucky enough, part of a sweet potato, their pockets stuffed full of the government's worthless paper currency, but they won't know that yet. Next to them will be their children too short to shoulder rifles, some Jews who have been banished all the way here from Warsaw but without the largesse of the Kadoories, the Ezras or the Sassoons, and younger mothers whose breasts are so dried up their babies are stunned, wasted and beyond crying. They are not in a privileged position to discuss the virtues between *collaboration* and *corroboration*. Theirs is the War of Infinite Resistance; they are the refugees moving from one devastated country to another devastated country, the ones scrounging for food and accepting daily compromises so their families will stay alive; their only enemy are those who break their promises to their mothers.

13

But what if the mother wasn't around to hug, remember and cherish those promises, that wingless gossamer of memory, bereft of time but inescapable?

Alone, the son was facing the barricade, stone in hand, a leftover from the last war two years ago. He might be lucky this time against these formidable odds and live to be captured and imprisoned before the International Red Cross has a chance. He had learned to survive torture and not give up anything by staying hungry so he would faint quickly, and to harbor such a deep hatred of the Japanese that he will muster enough stamina to endure that painful but temporary moment, as only a young boy can who has yet to learn how the idea of pain can be crippling.

On the other side of the street, a fresh detachment of marines had just arrived to bolster the barricade, their fingers itching inside the trigger guards of their mounted Vickers machine guns, the belts chockfull, threaded and locked. Their captain came chauffeured by armed motorcycle escorts, four in the front and two in the rear. They've settled into several downtown banks and department stores, cantonments against looters, insurgents, terrorists and lunatics alike, hermetically sealed and totally out of touch with the ground politic no more than fifty feet from their nearest feet. They had the bullet and the food, all that they need in the short run. Having been here for almost a decade, what was their short run? From one foreign concession abutted against another, time was running out during this ceasefire, but no one knew for sure for whom. In the name of their imperial flag the *Hinomaru*, they claimed they were here to liberate all Asia from centuries of European and American imperialism.

For now the boy with the stone in his hand was safe with everyone under the surveillance and ambiguous protection of the international Municipal Police, at least during daylight and depending on what flag they were waving, even the Confederate Battle Flag, a promotional souvenir from *Gone with the Wind* that just opened at the Grand. The boy also knew this was what it was like two summers ago, a nine year old when the earlier war began. He remembered seeing and hearing a swarm of carrier-based Imperial Navy dive-bombing Jeans which first appeared as noisy dots swooping down from the early rising sun over Shanghai, then less than a minute later as screaming bi-planes releasing their one-hundred-and-thirty-two pound high explosives and incendiaries from fifty feet, on civilian targets of no military consequence, except to terrorize, spread panic, maim and kill with sadistic devastation. And since their carriers the *Hōshō* and the *Ryūjō* were anchored just five minutes away where the Huangpu River confluenced with Suzhou Creek, these Yokosukas returned at noon, and again late in the afternoon, this time accompanied by strafing Nakajima escorts.

These sorties were followed a month later by the carpet bombing Mitsubishi Nell medium bombers based two hours away in Taiwan, dropping their 1,800 pound payloads along the tracks of the fleeing Generalissimo Chiang Kaishek first at Hangzhou, then Nanjing, and finally for two years round-the-clock at the itinerant capitol Chongqing.

The wounds from these bombing raids will scar the victims forever, a festering sore that will never heal. But for now Shanghai had settled down into the kimono of a ceasefire. The Paramount Ballroom on YuYuan Lu continued to provide a hedonistic nightlife, frequented mostly by men from the Japanese and German military and diplomatic corps and fast women after the quick buck. The smart ones were rumored to have left the city and were last seen holding out, hunkered down in rural areas, where they had learned to dig first and look for food and water later. There they didn't have to fly any flag, like the Jewish immigrants who had been chased out of every European country and Russia too, but were welcomed here where their children did not have to wear the Star of David and face the daily humiliation of the slurs and stares, except from other Europeans. Here they didn't have to struggle with which of the two sisters is a collaborator, each successive choice more restricted and dirtier than the last. Here, away from the ambient lights of the city especially when they were dimmed during air raids, from here they could clearly see the front side of the moon.

14

That was it, Ge thought back, sent to Beijing twenty years ago to cover the cultural pomp of Soviet President Mikhail Gorbachev's historic state visit to China

On May 15 to mend the twenty-year political and economic rifts between the two communist nuclear powerhouses, the USSR and the PRC, and to wrIte about the Ministry of Culture orchestrating the political use of dance and music at the welcoming ceremony for Gorbachev held at the airport instead of the traditional T^2 that was occupied at the time by demonstrating students, three weeks before the Soviet-trained hydrologist Premier Li Peng was almost brought down to his knees for being a month late to a negotiation meeting requested by the Beijing Normal

University student Wu'erkaixi who thought he was a descendent of the brother of Jesus who led the Millennial Taiping Rebellion almost a hundred and forty years ago that resulted in more than twenty million deaths, before this dissident northwestern Uighur like the Tank Man in Chapter 3 or the barefoot and blind lawyer Chen Guangcheng in Chapter 26 had escaped to the United States on a Harvard Nieman fellowship or New York University or Columbia or Brandeis scholarship, three weeks before Li Peng, Deng Xiaoping and Yang Shangkun, after ordering the seasoned Thirty-Eighth Army of the PLA to open fire on the students, attempted to restore social harmony in the country by issuing an official Document 8 ban against using the three words in the English alphabet beginning with a T, *Taiwan, Tibet and Tiananmen,*

but because of approaching deadlines I had to return to Shanghai two weeks before things started falling apart for the students at T^2, so two weeks before the government initiated its ideological purification program that offered answers to questions that were never asked, Ge ended up filing a review of a piano recital at the Beijing Concert Hall and the impossibly ambitious program that included Schumann's *Kreisleriana* and Beethoven's Opus 111 instead, beginning with *The American pianist Sonny Ling* and describing his Schumann *as a concentration on patience, letting the lines sing as they were written, without improvisation—no soulful indulgence in nineteenth century melancholia or turbulent schizophrenia here—sustaining the octave legato of the dotted rhythms, the percussive finger-work of the sixteenth notes moving into the finale, then the subtle rhythmic changes of the last movement and without giving the audience a chance to applaud, Ling rushed right into the Chopin Mazeppa etude as if he were in enemy territory facing the mad catastrophic diaspora between war and revolution, returning in*

that colossal arpeggiated revenge, the diminished sevenths holding ev-
erything together in the left hand, and again without waiting for the ap-
plause, Beethoven's last, the giant chords at the beginning a little detached
before the contrasting statements, letting the transitional cantabile *sing*
before the last, long variation, as if he had been waiting for it all his life,
ever so lightly, everywhere ever so lightly now, rotating his wrists into
the point-blank double and triple trills where all the notes turned to each
other in equal velocity, subdued, sharp and clear, into the expressive *short*
transition, letting it out here but again without indulgence, the only place
marked in the entire piece, and just as quickly, seamlessly, back to that
tranquil and unencumbered space, floating and distancing, lifting here in
compensation in these final semiquavers at the end of the piano, celebrat-
ing that solitude, and without regret, rising into that magnificent evapora-
tion, an ovation from a house still full at eleven p.m., well past the usual
nine p.m. final curtain Beijing audience expects, and without an encore, a
standing ovation and bravo, bravo, bravo and floral bouquets before Cao
Feng of the conservative *China Daily* wrote his more restrained review,
before Ge took a cab out to the airport on the new 3rd Ring Road thinking
about the political implications behind the utilitarian name *Ring Road,* as
if it reflected the language's ability to conceal, protect and create harmony, convinced it was another attempt to impose order on an urban culture
becoming more disorderly and fragmented and random by the day, and if
writers were doing the exact opposite, using language to divulge, interpret,
and explode, in a tense that is the present, the past, and the future all at
once, and how he's instead beginning an innocuous piece on what young
college-educated women in Beijing are reading, those who had taken a
comparative literature course as part of their requirement for an English
major based on the American educational model and were required to read
Leo Tolstoy's *Anna Karenina*, Cao Xueqin's *Dream of the Red Chamber*,
and Theodore Dreiser's *Sister Carrie* and had not thrown themselves under a bullet train to Shanghai.

15

They are reading novels, and a lot of them, Ge begins his article, *and many of them are writing their own and publishing them online where others can read them for free most of the time. They are not interested in the political novel, especially those that reveal malfeasance and corruption in business, government and the bedroom. And they are definitely not interested in love stories: they've had enough of that in Anna and Vronsky, Baoyu and Daiyu, George and Carrie, Mu Bai and Shu Lien, and Romeo and Juliet, even on the seventh day of the seventh month in the lunar calendar. As in the American Chick Lit novel-and-movie* Waiting to Exhale *(minus the sex), they begin full of girlish purrs, but end in failures of, of...* and here Ge is stumped; he wants to write *of the human heart,* but he knew Mr. Editor would delete it with his red or blue pencil or permanently by pressing a key on his laptop. Instead he writes, *Like the American writer Sophie Kinsella's gals who meet weekly at the shopping mall to lunch and shop, ours are also exchanging social platform identities, sharing apartment possibilities, career enhancement options, the latest* ifc mall *promotional for soap at Hermes or shoes at Vuitton, and which Taiwanese business to avoid, even if it's in the French Concession or under the watchful eye of Pudong's Oriental Pearl.*

Identifying the kidnapper, pickpocket, scoundrel, rake, rat or mole from an honest person on Nathan Road in Hong Kong, or on Nanjing Lu on the other side of the river from the Pearl in Shanghai in Ge's story now, that's almost impossible seventy years ago, especially with Dai Li's untrustworthy informants' help when we don't know their financial, ethical or political agenda, or if they were just ordinary residents pointing their personal finger for good ol' familial revenge or reestablishing clan harmony, or that nonchalant looking gal perched at the Zhongshan Long Bar with her Toni-permed wave and tight, knee-high red *qipao*, her Cuban cigar smudged a dark scarlet from her passion lipstick, still scheming to collect that hundred for doing it both ways. For now she's deciding if she wants to go to a matinee showing of *Gone with the Wind* at the Grand a block away, or a longer walk in her platforms to the Dai Sun on Nanking for some shopping with her five-finger discount.

In the meantime Ge is still struggling with his movie review that he didn't want to write in the first place, his attention focused on the only story of interest in his two years as a cub reporter covering the Settlement's Municipal Police blotter. Under intense interrogation at the SMP's Bubbling Well Station, a young pickpocket suspect had confessed to learning his techniques at the legendary School of Seven Bells outside Bogotá. It didn't make any sense, Ge thought, the guy must be lying. If he had really been to that school, he would never have given up this confession unless, unless of course he had been booted out for getting too high from his smoking pot at the eight-thousand-plus-some elevation of the Andes.

The pickpocket suspect had been nabbed outside the Baptist Church on Avenue Pétain working solo on a late Sunday morning far from the crowded Nanking Lu shoppers, marking a worshipper outside the front gate in her most vulnerable moment, with a crying toddler in tow while opening her purse to give him some of the paper currency left over from her weekly tithing. He was finally released on a technicality by the Sikh desk sergeant, since he had not actually filched anything from her. Sympathetic to the long Chinese tradition of how some Buddhist and Taoist monks in their resistance against the corrupt government have provided sanctuary in their monasteries to such criminals as thieves and the politically malcontent, he tore up both the booking sheet and the duty officer's interrogation authorization.

Such is the midnight cry of an occupied city between several wars, splayed out between indolence and longing.

16

Intrigued by the SMP brief description of the incident in front of the church, Ge looked over his notes again, convinced there were several layers of stories he wanted to uncover and write about. He wanted to interview the Sikh desk sergeant, but since that was impossible at that moment, he had a beer instead at the bowling alley with a trusted Fudan classmate, a journalist working at the Xinhua district office, both conveniently located only a couple of blocks from the church. In spite of the state's ownership and strict control of this news agency with its vast network of managed news for all the radio and television stations in China, the news magazines, Xinhuanet, and the two major English language newspapers, he believed his friend had been doing good work before his finished pieces were savaged and altered on the editors' computers.

From his friend he found out that this Baptist Church built in 1925 in this French Concession had changed its name to the inter-denominational Community Church less than twenty years ago, and was now nestled into a spacious lot with shade trees, across the street from the American Consulate and a Starbucks on what used to be the Avenue Pétain—so named by a Francophone consulate general in honor of his country's World War I hero who was later vilified for his fascist anti-Semiticism and felony-of-opinion laws during the next war and then tried for treason at its end—that had been changed to Hengshan Lu.

After perhaps too many beers, his friend added that this was also the church that California's 14-term lawmaker Nancy Pelosi and New Jersey's pro-life 17-term Chris Smith, first elected in the same year as Ronald Reagan's first presidency, came to worship and socialize when they were in town two years ago on a stopover before continuing to Beijing on their Congressional junket to honor the student protesters killed at T^2 in the political spring of 1989.

And one more thing, he added while Ge checked his cellphone app to match the taxi at curbside to take his friend home on a busy Saturday night, did you know Chinese people closest to the Americans are the wealthiest people in the whole damn country, starting with Madame Chiang Kaishek and her Steinway CD or Bösendorfer or whatever-dwarf and her two private DC3s or C-47s or whatever?

Forewarned of the crowd, Ge got to the church at six the next morning, a good hour before the service was scheduled to begin at 7:00, the first of the three in Chinese every Sunday. The thunderous hymnal singing was audible a good block away, and by the time Ge got to the gate, the congregation had already completely filled the four hundred seats in the main church as well as the six hundred in the upstairs of the attached auxiliary building that housed the Sunday school and nursery downstairs. The minister was welcoming the worshippers who continued to arrive, mostly women in small groups, some with young children, as well as older, single, retired men, who walked as if they were Baptists or Mormons focused on their mission. Ushers and elders were quickly setting up plastic chairs for the overflow in front of the bookstand outside the main building.

Ge walked over and looked over the titles of the books, most of them in English, and wrote them down in his notebook, *The Pilgrim's Progress, 1 Corinthians, 2 Corinthians, How to Conquer Depression, Caring for the Chronically Ill, How to be a Hero to Your Kids*. He picked up John R.W. Scott's *The Cross of Christ* and *The Contemporary Christian*, and jotted *British, world evangelist*, Time's *list of 100 most influential persons in the world.* A sign in English next to the bookstore announced the time for the two Sunday services in English open to foreigners with passports or resident permits, at two and four in the afternoon, and a reminder of what the Nebraska Senator Kenneth Wherry said when the war was finally over: *With God's help, we will lift Shanghai up and up, ever up until it is just like Kansas City,* a statement that defied translation.

Ge went outside the gate to look for the pickpocket from Bogotá and the woman perhaps an immigrant Uighur with her crying toddler, but they were not to be seen in the clamor of the intense traffic on Hengshan Lu or Avenue Pétain or anywhere on either side of the river, in Shanghai or out, as if they had never existed at all. Saddened, *Xīténg*, somewhere between sympathy and empathy, Ge felt the need to write about this in one form or another. But first he'll need some help from his Xinhua friend who has some access to the SMP's surveillance tapes to find those two last seen in front of the church.

17

This was where Bogotá Pickpocket and the Uighur Mother arranged to meet with Ge, at the Foreign Languages Bookstore on a side street recessed from Fuzhou Lu. Unlike those black surveillance cameras in the Bank Of China branch across the street, there were none here to capture these two who seem to have completely disappeared from both the police and the church.

Ge walked right up to them by the Chick Lit section and without pausing to find out if they were willing to be interviewed or asking them to sign a release permission slip, he asked his first question, Where's your crying toddler?

The Uighur mother without the baby paused, averted her eyes, and said she had returned her. In her halting Mandarin she continued. I borrow from friend, for my disguise you know, get past army men at American compound across street from church. I doing fine, until this dude here, she said, jabbing a finger into his jacket, this clumsy dude interrupted everything. Police man asked, I showed forged ID card you know; it was very expensive and crying child kept me from police station to go sign complaint. Policeman, nice man, not like most Chinese.

And you, you, she jabbed her finger at Double Dude harder this time. Where did you learn to work like that, shame on you. You must come out to my country sometime. We have school for fools like you, you know.

Ge started scribbling in his notebook. He was not going to let this moment slip by, the subjects interviewing each other, given that he wanted to get their stories right, word for word, and everything in between, everything.

And where is your country, Double Dude asked. You're not Chinese—he paused, as if waiting for a translator—that much I know from the way you talk.

Yes, you go as far west before you reach Tibet, right there. They no Chinese either.

But the Chinese claim both, as well as Taiwan and the rest of those islands; they wrap their contour around everything that's left on the drawing board.

They can claim what they want, but we no Chinese, ever. We kicked their butts during Tang Dynasty years ago, then begged us help them put down rebellion.

Tired of this interview, she picked up a book from the shelf behind her and continued. See this, I don't know enough English understand inside, this cover, see, this cover you know, fancy dress, very short, how do you say it, *Sex and the City*? This like China now, no? No job for my family, no money. Hans have much money, greedy merchants. They throw away.

Too much money, too much time, Double Dude echoed. They have no job for me either, and I am Han.

At this point Ge scratched out some words in his notebook and added new ones to the interview. *Designer clothes. Euro trash. Tourist trash. All the good stuff in Shanghai gone. Dance. Music. Books. Paintings. No one remembers any of it. Cultural suicide. China owes its citizens big time, but no one is paying. The bill is left unpaid.* Scratched out again.

What did you say, he interrupted them.

Wonderful, beautiful country in some places, Double Dude repeated, but terrible nation and some very terrible people in it, everyone, everyone with whatever passport or identity or party membership card they are carrying that day. That's why I pretend I went to school in Bogotá every morning when I get ready to live another day.

> For the human rights record today, the government produces ethnic appreciation videos with Han Chinese dressed in various tribal costumes—Miao, Zhuang, Kazakh or Uighur—singing nationalistic songs in Mandarin. Like De La Mer's *Miracle Broth* that resists aging, these visuals seen in commercials all over China's media venues, especially on the huge walls leading into T², become the assimilationist's super glue to make everyone look alike, that is, before they are made invisible and their land robbed of everything on it, above it and below it, except those few isolated reserves permitted to traffic in Made-in-Tséghahoodzání/Window Rock-Arizona colorful clothing, turquoise earrings and assorted Tibetan chic to support the tourist industry of the conquer, occupy and exploit model. The Miao, Zhuang, Kazakh and Uighur are represented in the southern city Shenzhen's China Folk Culture Village theme park in which residents mimic the daily lives of their imagined cultures, similar to the Polynesians' performance in the Mormon Temple in Oahu, Hawaii, the latter to the accompaniment of the C Major Prelude of Bach's *The Well-Tempered Clavier* played on a harp.

Uighur Mother and Bogotá Man had put their ears to the ground and planted their words into a few of the books in the store, some of them with Ge's compost addition. Peggy has said both language and the mind are not dependable. That remains to be seen; that remains to be seen, who'll buy one of these books, and if they'll pay any attention to what they are reading instead of suspecting it's just a trick of the author pretending omniscience.

18

No more words, he said, no more words, you must have action, he said and slapped a hand on the table for emphasis before translating it into German and then plain Chinese. *Aktion*, how do you say it in Chinese, *dóngzuó*?

Kuifang and Ge were having a late drink at the lavishly symmetrical Majestic Hotel on the Bund around the corner from his newspaper office. They were both listening to the strained accents coming from the two men at the candle-lit table next to them.

What is it, Ge whispered.

What is it right, *ma*? A bit of German, some Shanghai wu, a pinch of Mandarin? More like, who are they *ma*?

The four men with earbuds and bulging tunics at the table next to them looked menacingly at Kuifang and Ge, who were trying to appear as casual as possible and definitely minding their own business.

Ge reached out a hand for Kuifang's. Look out, he said quietly. Let's smile and act starry-eyed for the camera. Don't look now, but I recognize them, especially the quiet one on your left, the guy with the wig.

Kuifang raised her glass, swirled the ice and spoke quietly into it, hiding her voice. I do too, too, the glass echoed. That dapper guy has on a wig to cover his always-shaved peanut head, funny with a head full of black hair falling over his ears. His neck's straight, sitting upright, maybe a back problem *ma*?

And that's his German drinking buddy, Alex von Falken something.

No, that can't be, I thought Berlin pulled him back two years ago. She waved for a waitress and took a peek. Shit, you're right.

Can you hear what he's saying?

Yes, but I don't understand it. It's not German. Not English. Some kind of Chinese dialect. He's from Jhejiang, and those barbaric pirates have never had to learn Mandarin, or Shanghai wu either. Their men face north and piss at Beijing and Shanghai. Some Methodist missionaries up here speak better Mandarin.

The waitress is pretending she doesn't see me waving—no way, not in this fancy Majestic. But safer for her not to come over.

Let's go to another bar where we can talk then.

They got up slowly and walked across the hotel's legendary symmetrical four-leafed-clover grand ballroom that had held the reception for the three thousand guests at Chiang's marriage to Mayling Soong, including half the officers above the lieutenant commander rank of the American Seventh Fleet in full dress whites.

I don't believe this, Ge said aloud for both of them, another martini in his hand, this one without an olive at his insistence. You know Kuifang, I'll have to write this.

Yeah, but no one's going to publish it, or everyone will be executed, you, your editor, the fact checkers and the copy editor, the galley staff, the publisher, the typesetters, the printers, the ink boy, the delivery boys, the newsstand vendors, and all their families, even your grade school teacher and the man who cut down the tree for the paper, maybe everyone and their families and friends beheaded in the public square or football stadium, more than a thousand heads, to teach a lesson not to do it again maybe, like that emperor back middle of the eighth century Tang Dynasty who beheaded everyone who had anything to do with the courtier who had written something offensive about him in an improvident metaphor, the final execution held at the public market of the City of Perpetual Peace, Chang'an, taking more than three thousand heads in all for all to see and learn.

You're right, again. Like his banner year 1927.

And in his mind Ge started writing the piece anyway, carefully jotting down notes along the way, so he won't miss anything later just in case he'll ever have a chance to actually write it.

That's a good title, Banner Year: 1927. Sign it Renyuan. Chiang Kaishek started his year by hiring a voice coach, and diligently practiced Mandarin by speaking into a mirror and lip-synching Beijing talk radio programs, sometimes assisted by a wire recorder.

He wanted to accomplish two things that year, to muffle the communist CCP and break up their unions, and to marry Mayling Soong.

The first was easy to do, after luring them into Shanghai in April with promises of unification and then massacring them and their union sympathizers.

The next was more complicated, as it required getting divorced first—his intended's family were Methodists who frowned on polygamy. The matriarch Mammy Soong insisted on a divorce as a condition for her Youngest Daughter's Hand, as well as Chiang's religious conversion. Ever the promiscuous ideologue who believed whatever he wanted to believe and ally to anyone who'll Cash His Check, Chiang was promptly baptized. In a sartorially decorated fresh uniform, spats, black cutaway and a sword in hand, he was baptized by the Reverend Z.T. Kaung at the Young Allen Methodist Church in Shanghai, with the heavily armed thugs of the Green Gang providing security, frisking everyone and confiscating all their weapons, except for the American military attachés and their Admiral Mark Bristol acting as witnesses, who refused to check their Colt 1911s at the door.

Soon Chiang appeared in another new uniform on the cover of *Time*, an American newsweekly owned by the son of Methodist missionaries Henry Luce, a *mishkid* who also owned *Life*, *Fortune*, and *Sports Illustrated*. In the following years the Chiangs were to appear more than ten times on the covers of these magazines, separately and together.

Later he appeared in disguise in a wig, alone except for the same but older Green Gang bodyguards, at the same hotel where a White Russian orchestra played Mendelssohn's *Wedding March* transposed to the higher key of D to accommodate the ten bamboo flutes—a wedding gift from his home province in the south, Jhejiang—and an American tenor sang *Oh Promise Me* for his wedding reception twelve years earlier. It was rumored that Madame Chiang was on sabbatical in Chongqing at the time and supervising the shipment of her two Steinway CDs and getaway stash of 400-ounce gold ingots, as well as making sure her personal army of women with cowboy hats were not seduced by the Flying Tiger mercenaries flying protection, paid or volunteer like John Wayne in a movie two years later.

He was accompanied by his trusted German adviser General Alexander von Falkenhausen, who was rumored to be conspiring with his friend Field Marshall Erwin von Witzleben in planning a coup d'état against the *Führer*. The two of them appeared to be arguing over political and military strategy and whether to use the Lend-Lease weapons now against the Japanese or hoard them to fight off the communists at the end of the war, as surely the Americans were eventually going to enter the war and blow out the rising sun of the enemy.

Ge, Ge, Kuifang repeated impatiently. You're not listening. You're writing that piece in your head *ma*?

Yes he was, on the opposite side of the street from those master calligraphers freelancing red door posters that embraced the imagined cyclical rhythms of the seasons and the pearly words of wisdom filched from ancient proverbs, to ward off spiritual evil for both domestic and foreign consumption, but ignoring the scars of poverty and violent repression by both the state and family, with numbing consequences almost impossible to reverse even before these aphorisms were tattooed onto the arms of circus, naval and biker desperadoes and stitched onto the bodies of the American N.F.L. and N.B.A. players who won't have a clue what these words mean.

Oh, promise me that someday you and I
Will take our love together to some sky
The human heart is hard to grasp
You get what you pay for

19

The next thing we know, the two of them were having a beer at the bowling alley on Avenue Pétain across the street from the Baptist Church where Bogotá Pickpocket was arrested a week ago.

Something's not right here, Mr. Ge, we need drums, drums, a lot of them for celebrating this Festival of the Emperor's Last Fish.

Yes, Mr. *Páshǒu*, you're right there. Three hundred beats to announce the festival, three hundred exactly. Tradition, count them, all the way to the last carp in the emperor's pond or in the dumplings on his table.

They laughed at the word play that'll be a challenge for the translator and asked for more, their fingers tapping the tabletop as if it were a drum.

After many beats, maybe three hundred of them exactly, Ge asked, Will you tell me, without lying, did you really learn your trade up in the Andes?

Bogotá *Páshǒu* stroked his chin as if he had a beard. Yes, but only if you give me your word you won't write about it. He paused, waiting for the translator. Off the record only, he emphasized. And put away your notebook.

After waiting some more, he added, What's the use. You're going to do it anyway, sooner or later, maybe disguised in fiction, no? So get out your notebook: at least get it right.

Ge said No, no, I don't do fiction, and tucked his notebook back into his jacket pocket and ordered two more beers, and more as the festival celebrations picked up.

Páshǒu admitted to having been to Bogotá, but that's getting ahead of the story.

He had grown up near Ice City. His parents were not merchants and did not own any land, but as school teachers they earned just enough to send all their children to school. His interest in pickpocketing developed when he read a translation of *Oliver Twist* in middle school, three times, he said, his copy underlined, page corners dogeared and all. Not that he wanted to be a professional pickpocket, he assured Ge, he just wanted to learn what it's like to make something next to someone's body disappear and they didn't even know it. A class act. Panache. No knives or guns. Just a light touch, *poco a poco, pianissimo.*

A classmate told him South Americans were the best pickpockets in the world. Shanghai, Hong Kong and Guangzhou had schools and all, but nothing like those in Colombia or Brazil, especially the legendary school high up in the Andes, the School of Seven Bells.

With enough money borrowed from friends and relatives on the pretext of going around the world to find his way in life, he set sail for Cartagena through the Panama Canal and climbed onto an open truck on an unimproved dirt road a night and a day and eight thousand feet up to the school inside a monastery outside Bogotá and laid down his tuition, admit me please, I am all the way from China, he said in his memorized Castilian Spanish he had learned from the tramp steamer Filipino Third Mate on his three-week voyage over the Pacific.

A monastery, Ge asked, and started to take out his notebook.

Yes, a monastery, and put that notebook back in your pocket. At least have the courtesy to do it from memory.

No, no, Ge explained. Look at him, look at his tattoos, he nodded to the CrossFit carnie displaying his bulging triceps in a sleeveless performance tee who had just sat down two tables away. I'm writing down his English-word tattoos.

Second Mortgage. Disinterment. Fornificate. Something went wrong in the translation?

Like the other way, the three most requested Chinese words that went south in American tattoo art: snake—*shé*, luck—*yùnqì*, strength—*shīlì*.

See why I don't do fiction? How can you beat that!

They laughed again, at how language deceives, reveals and confuses before ordering more beers and continuing with the Bogotá story.

After six months of classes with demonstrations and field work in town, the half-blind Master Monk with one glass eye gave the new class their final examination. M^2 was legendary for inventing a solo in lifting money out of a woman's purse while she was going through a revolving glass door at the NYC Broadway Bloomingdale's when she was going in and he was going out to hail a taxi. All the apprentices did well in the team challenges, performing a variety of distractions and relays, but *Páshǒu* had some problems in the solo final. He had the poise, steadiness and patience and passed the test without ringing any of the seven bells lining M^2's seven pockets when he emptied them of their valuables, but his high altitude nosebleed left a trail of blood obvious enough for any amateur to track even in the busy, dusty public square.

You must be careful, M^2 warned him as he climbed up the same truck for a ride down to Cartagena for his return voyage to Shanghai, or they will catch you, believe me.

Then why did you get nabbed while working such an easy mark in front of a church, a trusting Christian mother with toddler in tow and a purse carelessly left wide open?

Páshǒu stroked his beard carefully before answering. I wasn't mindful that she had a borrowed baby whose crying stopped me cold. Loud alarm. Everyone looked my way, including that cop. That's why they didn't find anything on me. I had stopped when the toddler started crying. You have met the mother. She's a Uighur; should have known she wasn't a Han from her dark skin.

He did stop then and after, deciding instead to change his life to become a professional bridge player, a C.P.A. maybe, maybe enrolling at Fudan and getting a college degree in ethics even when most of the university had already moved upriver to an interior tributary of the Yangtze and away from the war.

20

I tried explaining to him why I don't do fiction, Ge explained to Kuifang.

The two of them were having dinner at the Old Station on CaoxiBei Lu in the attached Russian railway carriage that had belonged to one of the three Soong sisters, Chingling, the wife of the original theoretician of China's 20th century revolution, Sun Yatsen. For a look at the old colonial atmosphere, Kuifang had suggested last week, and trying out the traditional Shanghai lake shellfish recipe, so different from my Xi'an restaurants' more ambitiously colored and gentle cuisine. Restored from a Jesuit monastery in the French Concession from almost a century ago, same period as that Baptist Church you've been telling me about with that pickpocket and Uighur woman with the borrowed baby. Not far from your bowling alley on Hengshan.

Hey Kuifang, you're not listening, like when I was explaining it to him.

Kuifang apologized. I couldn't stop looking at that portrait of Jesus Christ there, she pointed, on the wall to your left, between the two antique gramophones. Okay, okay, I'll pay attention. What explanation *ma*?

Mr. *Páshǒu* had been nudging me toward writing his story in fiction and I was explaining to him why I don't do fiction.

Yes, you've told me that before—many times—as a journalist you're in the business of reassuring your readers, you verify, sometimes explain and blame, like the pimp of certainty you once said. I think you're becoming a moralist.

Ge started working on his hairy crab with both hands. And why not, he said, why not, when everyone else is busy being a dissident in public, but in the privacy of their homes they are rushing to contact and collaborate with their handlers at the Brown Shirts, Green Gang or Desert Camo. This is quite good, especially the wine and the ginger. Yours? Adding, We don't give the readers anything at all, not really. Not even the weather reports that we pilfer from the military and dress up nice and fluffy for public consumption. Fifty percent chance for rain, we're covered either way, like Mao Zedong is 60/40 correct. The cops got the alleged killer, we report, as if we're heralds of the criminal justice system. You can go shopping at the mall again. That's all they want to hear and stay comfortably drugged like they were in high school history class. Besides that, most journalists can't even write a sentence.

This is really good, this powdered crabmeat and tofu. She said she might try to infuse parts of these culinary embellishments into the menu at one of her restaurants. That might prompt some of those Taiwan businessmen to take their wives out to dinner once in a while and stop their fucking shenanigans with my staff.

And what else did you say to him *ma*, she continued, serving both of them some accompanying thick Shanghai noodles stir fried with bok choy and yellow onions, and some sautéed fresh shrimp laced with wine and lime.

You know, I'd like to write food for the paper sometime, you know? Mr. Editor and I will argue again. He'd say the paper has a foodie editor already, and I will say that food also comes under culture, and I'm the culture writer, no?

Then what would you have to say about this Shanghai cuisine at this restaurant?

Oh, that'll be easy. A lot of liquor, ginger, lime, and especially shellfish from the lakes around here, not renowned for its subtleties. Acceptable service. Colonial ambiance. Clean tables, and no soy sauce in sight.

Ge, for sure Michelin's not going to hire you, a pity. You've got to do a lot more than that to convince those who hate Shanghai cooking, who prefer the spicier Sichuan dishes and claim that Shanghai cooking is nothing more than steamed bottom riverfood peppered with waste washed four thousand miles down the Yangtze River from the Tibetan Plateau glaciers, and that you have to eat its most famous dish with both hands like a barbarian *ma*?

You got me, Ge laughed. I've been found out. But don't tell Mr. Editor, he doesn't need any help arguing with me. Actually, I was still thinking about journalism, and how a critic of Ah Zee's piece in that Beijing newspaper last week prompted him to say that people who cast their votes based on what they've read in the newspaper should have their right to vote taken away. Maybe do an op-ed piece for Mr. Editor, about how we journalists provide a public service and invent heroes for our nascent values, like that American iconic and Pulitzer-winning photograph of their marines' staged raising of their victorious flag over Iwo Jima's Mount Suribachi in February of forty-five, always looking for a happy ending, even those historians straining to find a kernel of goodness in Robert McNamara who had authored the Gulf of Tonkin Resolution that brought the United States officially into the war in Vietnam in 1964, leading to nearly two decades of murderous atrocities including the ten-year deployment of the weapon of mass destruction, Monsanto and Dow Chemical's Agent Orange resulting in intergenerational degenerative physical, mental and cultural disabilities.

What I want to know, she asked as she dipped into their dessert of fresh tofu suspended in amber, spicy ginger syrup and spiked with peanut bits, what I want to know, did you ever find out why that Uighur woman needed to borrow a baby to get around the American Consulate, I mean, couldn't she just walk around that block *ma*?

That one's easy, that's what we do. Lost-and-Found. Aid and comfort to the middle class. First, the Uighurs have their way of doing things that sometimes confound us. Then there are those two police stations near the American Consulate to think about, two blocks away on each side of the compound, at Bubbling Well Lu and Gordon Lu, and they both have PLA surplus Norinco armored personnel carriers with mounted 107s. The Americans probably chose that site for their Consulate around 1982 during their President Ronald Reagan's war against drugs with the weapons and all for the freedom fighters, safer for them maybe.

As they walked past the Jesus Christ painting on their way out, Kui-fang nudged Ge and said, The tour guides recommend this restaurant for those who want a nostalgic look at old occupied, colonial Shanghai. More like looking at opulence and waste, don't you think, and on whose back *ma*?

21

You have that unfocused blank look about you, as if you're having a conversation with yourself *ma*, Kuifang asked next morning at breakfast.

Do I? Ge looked puzzled. Maybe that's what we writers ever do, imagining a conversation with our characters, or an interview with Dai Li, journalist or novelist.

She leaned over, poured some more tea and whispered for him to be quiet about it, keep it in your head, she suggested. You never finished your story last night about your conversation with Mr. Bogotá, she added, sitting back down and straightening her sleeves.

That was the difficult part, Ge explained and looked over her shoulder at the sunrise. It involved everyone, and I mean everyone.

Here it is then, he continued. That conversation included the author, his translator, a linguist from Fudan, a literary theoretician from Yale, a Max Planck resident cultural anthropologist, the author's literary and subsidiary agents, the publisher, and Dai Li's personal emissary. And above all, reps from both the Bureau of Investigation and Statistics, and the State Administration of Press, Public Radio, Film and Television. And you, the reader.

That's what you were talking to yourself about *ma*?

Not just that, I was talking to everyone about why I can't do fiction. Too much emphasis on form, I need more space. Even Henry Fielding had more room back in the first quarter of the eighteenth century three hundred years ago, walking right into his novel as the author and having a self deprecating conversation with his readers.

I am convinced I never make my reader laugh heartily, but where I have laughed before him; unless it should happen at any time, that instead of laughing with me, he should be inclined to laugh at me. Perhaps this may have been the case at some passages in this chapter, from which apprehension I will here put an end to it.

At which point they got uppity, intense and abstract. The young literary agent said if you fuck around with the form, you're taking your life in your hands. The anthropologist believed form is a social function, a way of allowing the middle class to buy its way into culture, like books, paintings, movies and sonatas, a map to respectability and meaning. But I wasn't sure they were saying that. Look, I interrupted them. I was afraid of using a metaphor in the middle of their discussion of abstract ideas, because it might backfire or be taken as a senile detour, but I did it anyway. I said, Let's let the cat out of the bag, let's cut to the chase.

Locked into their think tank rhetoric, they directed their incredulous look at me, as if something had moved in the wastebasket. Form, form, I repeated. The A, B, and C of form in fiction. A is the exposition, the cat goes up the tree. B is the development, complications in getting the cat down from the tree. C is the recapitulation, the moral and comforting conclusion, the cat gets down from the tree, and all's well. That is all too much for me, too restrictive. And besides, where does the idea of form come from? Is it defined by maggots using dead models for their statistical abstraction, then insisting on its seismic propriety? Don't they see, they're telling us what to do, taking away our space for invention and room for making beautiful new things? At least the linguist and anthropologist were saying that form is a living thing, prone to changing its shape, rhythm and weave, borrowing and stealing, crossing over, not a static thing stapled to a church door. But the literary agent had the last word, You have to get the cat up the tree and you have to get it back down, period, or else you won't have a commercially viable manuscript, period.

And just before I left, I said as a writer I'm not interested in the fun beginning A or cheerful end C where the cat gets down and we can all go shopping at the mall again. I'm only interested in the B, the middle, the why and how to get the cat down, the part that Peggy said was *the stretch in between that's the hardest to do anything with.* They of course wanted to know who Peggy was. First I said Peggy Lee, but since they did not recognize her as the voice of Darling in *Lady and the Tramp*, I said she's that Toronto writer who imagined the novel *Oryx and Crake.*

And that was what you were talking to yourself about? For once Kuifang didn't end a question with her trailing *ma.*

Ge looked at her for a long moment. You've known all along, haven't you. How did you know?

At the way you've been distracted the last couple of months. Kuifang hesitated before continuing. At first I thought you were seeing a sweetie somewhere, but I knew better; you would tell me if you were. Then it wasn't long before it hit me because you were denying it too much. The more you denied it, the more I thought the opposite. Listen to you at dinner last night. I bet you are the author of the Ah Zee piece.

The reader has known this from the very beginning of Chapter 8, where the author had stepped out-of-bounds to reveal what he had found when he hacked into Ge's MacBook Pro, the lead paragraph set in Century Gothic font to show such an intrusion, such as this one.

That's probably why you didn't convince your friend Mr. Bogotá at the bowling alley last week *ma*?

Ge smiled, relieved that at least he did not have to continue his deception with Kuifang. Yes, he admitted, he did write that Ah Zee piece, with the reference to Lu Xun, and thanked him for the first paragraph and what he said in the last.

Kuifang finished her tea, and embraced Ge before leaving for the Bank Of China branch on Fuzhou Lu to see about securing an advance to launch her fourth Xi'an restaurant in Shanghai.

But Ge was not all there, again. He was thinking he must write something about all those huge public statues of Mao Zedong all over China's urban landscape, especially in Beijing, where he counted nine of them just in a small section of the University District alone. The first one was bad enough, but they all looked like duplications made from the same mold, except they were of different sizes, S, M, L, XL, and, he found out, the new one outside the medical university in Chongqing, XXXL.

Mao has already been officially downgraded from being 100 percent correct to 60/40, so maybe his monuments should reflect this contentious historical debate, since public statues are after all symbols that unite us and explain ourselves to others, true or not, like it or not. He had also heard that the runaway province one hundred miles on the east side of the Black Ditch has been having similar revisionist thoughts of their leader Chiang Kaishek when they moved all his public memorials to an enclosed dump miles from the capital, and closed his museum and archives to the public. At the same time Xinhua, China's official news agency of the central government that promulgates its policies globally, has been publishing stories that Chiang was maybe not all bad, that some of his legacy is redeemable. No stone is going to be left unturned. Start digging. Nothing is set in stone.

This was all getting too much for Ge; he had to write something about it, maybe another short story, and sign it Renyuan to keep his job.

22

Ge believed that like his non-fiction culture writing, the factual sections of his fiction must be accurate enough to pass the paper's scrupulous
fact checker's scrutiny as well, unless I get bored, he said to himself, before titling the story "Cultural Exchange."

Ever since Generalissimo Chiang Kai-shek expatriated
himself to Taiwan in 1949 after a protracted civil war, his en-
tourage and the victorious Chairman Mao Zedong have been
tormenting each other over China's identity in all of its Ponzi
derivatives, unraveling a shifting political and cultural landscape of revenge and justice, with the U.S. 7th Fleet wearing
a referee's black-and-white and patrolling the South China

Sea's Black Ditch between them to promote world peace. Occasionally they would take errant shots at each other over the hundred miles of water separating them, an Extravagant Burst here, a Vibrant Crackle there, Sparklers and Snakes everywhere, until the American aircraft carrier *USS Hornet* slipped in between them with its Rockets' Red Glare. That is, until the two coots General Cash My-check and Old Garlic Breath died within a year of each other and shortly after the *Hornet* was decommissioned the third and last time in 1970, initiating an amorphous detente between the People's Republic of China and Taiwan, and that was more than thirty years ago.

> Nice. Thanks for the history lesson. But that was then, this is now. What is now, and where's the story? Even a parable has a story line. Come on, get that damn cat up the fucking tree, Mr. Storyteller.

At about the same time, the electronic surveillance systems of international intelligence networks hummed with the traffic that the Canadian munitions engineer Jerry Bullock who had built the largest cannon in the world for Iraq's Saddam Hussein might be for hire. A dozen spy agencies including the British MI-6, USA's CIA, Iran's VEVAK, Israel's Mossad, USSR's KGB, France's Deuxième Bureau, and Japan's PSIA tried to pick up his mortgage in exchange for his cannon designs, or at least to poison him to exempt his mercenary services from their enemies.

Through its secret service section of the Ministry of State Security, the Chinese found the Canadian hiding out in the chess champion Bobby Fischer's former apartment on Espergerdi Street in Iceland's capital Reykjavik and learning to play chess from the scribbled notes left by Bobby Fischer, and talked him into building another cannon, for old time's sake, just one last one, this one won't kill anyone, it'll just be symbolic, like most people's lives. And it will be easy.

Nobody would have guessed at the time Pythagoras worked out his Triples Theorem $a^2 + b^2 = c^2$ amended two centuries later by Euclid's Infinite Series, $(3n)^2 + (4n)^2 = (5n)^2$ that it would be hijacked into the mathematical centerpiece for calculating ballistic trajectories in a shooting war between China and Taiwan some two-thousand-and-five-hundred years later. At least this was what the cannon enthusiast wearing a card dealer's green visor was explaining to the People's Liberation Army political officers hunkered down over a ping-pong table in a mobile command center parked on a rock-lined beach on Quemoy Island, just a short sand wedge shot from Taiwan.

In the last twenty years, memories of the 1989 political spring and the Tiananmen[2] confrontations had been quietly shelved and dwarfed by the rapid economic growth of entrepreneurial capital showcased in the construction of the Three Gorges Dam on the Yangtze River, Beijing hosting the Olympics, and Shanghai's 2010 Expo. The 21st century was beginning to look like it belonged to China, its Dragon Century. During this period Taiwan had become more of an economic partner than a political adversary when it sent 400,000 businessmen to summer camp in Shanghai, all the while procuring huge quantities of munitions from everyone, including more than one-hundred-and-fifty Falcon F-16 attack fighters from the U.S. alone, just in case.

During this same period on the mainland, Mao icons, statues, talismans, memorials and memorabilia both public and personal became anachronistic, along with his reputation, at least in the prosperous coastal free economic zones. First, the party officially admitted Mao had erred in some of his political and personal decisions and writings, but he was still 90% correct, though no one knew for sure which was the 90 and which was the 10. A few years later his ratings were downgraded to 80. Then 75. Then 70. Then 60 last year. PLA uniform Mao badges converted to fashionable earrings started appearing in Shanghai nightclubs, first on women, then on men; first on both ears, then on one, both left and right. Taxi drivers in busy cities threw away their Mao talismans believed to ward off accidents. His image was deleted from sports trophies and chess and bridge championship medals. School children started to forget his name, even when his image ran amok on every piece of paper currency in the country from one Yuan to a hundred, even with the 12.26 meters high, identical public Mao statues in plaster, gypsum, stone, bronze or stainless steel everywhere, everywhere. [The statue itself is 7.1 meters, to correspond with the founding of the Chinese Communist Party on July 1, 1921; and the base is 5.16 meters, to commemorate the publication date of "Guidelines for the Cultural Revolution" on May 16, 1966.]

Merchants started complaining. Not good for tourism. College students, independent newspaper editorials and intellectuals started complaining. Bad memory; this is not China today.

Some radical officers in the PLA and senior cadres in the CCP started fomenting a plan, for the good of the country's public memory. Slowly one by one, week by week, these Mao statues started disappearing, especially from western Beijing's University District, even that recent supersized, twenty meters high and weighing forty-six tons stainless steel Mao at Chongqing Medical University's front entrance.

Since the cannon had been guaranteed to deliver a shell 1,500 miles, here the distance between Mainland's Quemoy and the beaches below Taichung across the Taiwan Strait, the distance was only 110. Easy. Piece of cake. More like a catapult. And besides, no ammunition would be involved, only the harmless public statues. Calibrating the trajectory (c^2) will be as easy as determining the hypotenuse of three points, squared or not: measure the distance between the two points at right angle to each other and then enter it into the computer along with the data on the length (a^2) and weight (b^2) of the projectile. In fact, the wireless link between the computer and the firing mechanism will also automatically calculate the current wind direction (a) and speed (b), and atmospheric variables such as humidity (($3n)^2$) and pressure (($4n)^2$). The only complication would be removing the Little Red Book (($5n)^2$) from Mao's hand on some of the statues, because its odd size would foul up the grooves in the barrel.

And by the time the US 7th Fleet responded by launching its Super Hornet attack fighters from the nuclear-powered super-carrier *USS George Washington* anchored in Tokyo Bay 1,500 miles away, or the Raptor interceptors from Guam 1,800 miles away, the show will be over. No one hurt—only Mao's feet sticking up in the air and his head buried in the sand of Taiwan's beaches.

Are we ready then, the senior PLA officer confirmed, looking down the long row of freight cars filled with Mao statues queued up on the same rail siding constructed to absorb the recoil of the brand new 100-foot long cannon barrel.

Unknown to him [and the rest of us], Taiwan had prepared itself for this paranoiac eventuality, and had been secretly building a similar cannon pointed at Quemoy's beaches.

ALEX KUO

Like China, Taiwan had been experiencing identical problems with Old Peanut Head icons, and had in fact been collecting all his public statues in full military dress with drawn saber and sometimes peacock plumage and storing them in an unmarked and bulging warehouse waiting for some evacuation plan, just like 1949 in reverse. And just like the PLA, a few Taiwanese military officers came up with the same idea, and with a less bureaucratic intelligence agency had in fact located the same Canadian engineer in Reykjavik a few months before the mainland spooks.

So, when the shooting started, the return fire was almost immediate, and the sustained exchange devastating. Statue after statue flew across the Taiwan Strait and landed as illegal aliens. Some collided in mid-air and exploded into dust, leaving no stone unturned. The noise disturbed residents as far away as Fuzhou and Taipei. Some counted the number of explosions like train cars, but stopped when they reached one hundred. Some remembered the 70s, when armies on both sides of the Taiwan Strait floated bundles of consumer goods to the other's shores in order to showcase its prosperity. Taiwan sent underwear, tape recorders, and biscuits embossed with Chiang Kaishek's image; and Mainland reciprocated with beef jerky, tea, and Moutai liquor.

Like fireworks displays, the shelling ended exactly thirty minutes from the start with a 72-shot Armageddon Brocade

Finale. For more than sixty years both China and Taiwan had wanted more, they wanted revenge and justice and another chance to fly its sovereign flag—the civil war was not over yet. Sometimes, just sometimes, justice is only a matter of distance; revenge however, is only a shortcut to nowhere.

Ge signed it Renyuan and sent it off to his editor as a PDF file before closing his laptop.

23

Most musicians Ge knew liked to tell rumors and moronic why-the-chicken-crossed-the-road jokes as if they were rehearsing a one-act 18th century Italian comic opera. At best they're not reliable informants or witnesses. They could be journalists, except they're more interested in the bizarre and the theatrical, perhaps to compensate for the regularity of much of their music, and the practice, practice, practice regimen of a caged animal, or a monkey whose neck's in the noose at the end of the organ grinder's tether.

Such was Ge's thinking when he took Line 7 to violinist Ning Feng's Shanghai recital at the brand new Shanghai Symphony Orchestra Hall on FuxingZhong Lu for his paper's weekend arts and entertainment insert. In addition to the press pass, he had also received a hand-scripted invitation for a post-recital reception at the French Concession home of SSO's new musical director Yu Long, the concurrent artistic director of both the China Philharmonic in Beijing and the Guangzhou Symphony.

Ge had selected a seat near the front and middle of the wrap-around seating in this magnificent recital hall designed by the innovative Arata Isozaki. Even though he did not play any musical instrument, he'd always wanted to face the musicians in such an intimate setting to look closely at the finger work of both the violinist and pianist. Seated early, Ge opened the glossy brochure to the evening's program.

Dimitri Shostakovich	Violin sonata, Opus 134
Arvo Pärt	Violin sonata Fratres
Erich Korngold	Much Ado about Nothing
Alexander Glazunov	Meditation
Niccolò Paganini	I Palpiti

Accompanied by Weicong Zhang on a Yamaha

The concert hall was filling up, and chatting students presumably from the nearby Shanghai Conservatory of Music with their iPhone 5ses launched just last week, iPads and Seven for All Mankind jeans with its swoosh embroidered on their butts climbed over him, *dàoqiàn, dàoqiàn.* A *China Daily* critic had estimated there were at least fifty million children in China taking piano or violin lessons, or both, but the conservatory's distinguished pianist and legendary teacher Madame Zhou Guangren had said in an interview with Ge last month that this fad will not last, it merely reflected a morphing middle class trying to define itself by buying its way into the bourgeoisie culture that they had been denied the last sixty years. Even the state was encouraging this recent acceptance of western classical music. It actively promoted the media and public adulation of the pianist Lang Lang as if he were a female panda bear about to give birth. But Mme Zhou said we have to be cautious here, and cited the story of the state enticing composer Chen Qigang into directing the contest-winning fifty composers writing music for the 2008 Beijing Olympics' global audience, adding, Sometimes we are our worst enemy when we censor ourselves to please the audience or keep our patrons.

At the end of the published interview, Ge focused on the prisoner's dilemma that while western countries are bemoaning the diminishing interest in its own classical music with the same small group of geriatric connoisseurs going from one concert to the next, the music halls in China were almost full every night with a rowdy younger audience in their 20s and 30s, some in their sequin-decorated tees and designer jeans.

Trying to ignore these talking and text-messaging youngsters, Ge flipped to the second half of the program that included an announcement of Mr. Ning's program next weekend in Hong Kong.

Wolfie Mozart	Violin sonata in G	K301
Ludwig Beethoven	Violin sonata in D	Op 30 No 3
Franz Schubert	Violin sonata in D	Op 137 No 1
Ludwig Beethoven	Violin sonata in D	Op 12 No 1

Accompanied by Weicong Zhang on a Steinway

Ge was amazed at the contrasting music between the Shanghai and Hong Kong programs. He saw that while the Shanghai pieces were all 20th century except for the Paginini, the Hong Kong were 18th century except for Schubert and Beethoven who found their way into the first quarter of the 19th, and jotted down some notes for his review. What pathological obsession in their familiarity with the classical and the romantic repertory as if no other music existed. No wonder the younger generations were flocking to indie rock, piano lesson or no piano lesson. The second program seemed tailored for the Hong Kong audience, a left-over from its colonial period during which the victims excelled at mimicking the politics and culture of their rulers down to the Steinway, and are still arguing among themselves after its return to China that was decided some thirty years ago whether Mandarin or the Guangdong dialect is the mother language. I'll have to add this to the long list of things I want to talk with PK about when I see him next month in Hong Kong at the Old Drunken Boat in Wan Chai.

In the meantime I need to work on Mr. Editor to make sure he's going to run this review of tonight's recital that's not going to sound like a press release from Mr. Ning's booking agent's press kit and its carefully balanced and restrained language to please both the media watchdogs as well as the expat culture vultures in Hong Kong.

24

Ge decided to walk slowly to the reception and let his memory randomly recall some details from Mr. Ning's recital, pausing at the astonishingly complex solo beginning of Arvo Pärt's *Fratres*, almost a minute-and-a-half of complicated writing mixing pianississimo and fortississimo within 64th notes arching over two bell-ringing octaves. He got out his notebook and under the streetlights jotted down some lines for his review. You've got to be insane to write or play that minimalist music, but I know Mr. Editor will delete this line. The notes were very clear, but the acoustics of the concert hall seemed to lack warmth, the sound prickly as if it had been digitized. The full house should have taken away some of that edge; maybe it's from the newness of the polished acoustical ceiling tiles, or maybe something else. Check this.

In the spacious living room of the musical director's home, Ge and the composer Xian Xinghai were having a lively conversation, each with at least a third glass of the lightning Maotai in hand. A gentle man, Xian said in his soft Mandarin, but Ge wasn't sure the accent was entirely southern, and thought he could hear some Portuguese or English downturns at the end of some of his vowels. Waving an imaginary baton, Xian was excited that Maestro Mario Paci had just approved his request to be the guest conductor of Shanghai Municipal Orchestra's Beethoven Eighth in the upcoming season, the first time a Chinese musician would step up to the podium.

A historical occasion, and about time, Ge added.

Nein, nein, nicht doch, Nur für Deutsche, the uniformed German military attaché insisted as he joined them.

Ge thought this officer was not only overbearing, pompous and loud, but his tunic barely covered his obesity. You can always spot a German in the crowded downtown Bund because they appear to be the only foreigners in China who have not lost any weight since their arrival.

Ge had seen him at Mr. Ning's violin recital earlier, someone not at all interested in the music who carefully shifted his attention away from the stage and worked the audience, pausing at other foreign military delegates, as if he were checking out the political calculus of the French, Japanese, and the Russians in East Asia.

Yes, he continued in English this time. German music for Germans, and Richard Wagner and Ludwig Beethoven the most German of German composers.

Ge imagined he could hear Goethe and his old pal Beethoven go ballistic at hearing his music used this way.

So, Xian interrupted, so, Ludwig Beethoven and I have much in common, although he could not get the *wig* in Ludwig quite right. Beethoven's mother was a helper in rich people's kitchens. So was mine.

We're talking about the music here and not about your *Mutter*, the German barked. Wagner now, he's another matter, not like the weak spirit of your Chinese sing sing. That's another matter entirely now, Richard Wagner for the Chinese impossible to understand, reversing the word order as he repeated louder the second time, impossible for the Chinese to understand Richard Wagner, as if he thought Ge and Xian could not understand English.

In 1932 the German composer Richard Strauss gave a speech in which he thanked Reich Chancellor Adolf Hitler and Reich Minister Dr. Goebbels for the revival of Germany's music culture. In that same year German violinist and conductor Gustav Havemann—early supporter of both Paul Hindemith and Arnold Schoenberg—consented to play with the Hamburg orchestra celebrating the birthday of Johannes Brahms only after insisting that all the Jewish musicians were to be removed from the orchestra, especially ironic when we are reminded that Brahms had objected to the same anti-Semitism directed against his friend Felix Mendelssohn more than a century ago. Havemann ended up performing to a nearly empty hall propped up by yawning Brownshirts from the Nazi Youth League.

You will never change your mind, will you, *Deutschland über alles*, Ge said and downed his fourth Maotai, and in the giddiness of the moment he just could not resist adding, You just will not forget the Fritz Kreisler incident when he came here on a concert tour a couple of years ago, will you. You don't want to see it repeated.

That never happened, the officer attaché looking straight at Ge. What nonsense are you talking about?

Well, I see by the three gold bars on your sleeves, Mr. *Korvettenkapitän,* Xian said quietly in his native Cantonese, after Mr. Kreisler learned that we were not allowed into his SMO concerts, he played the next afternoon in a movie theatre for the Chinese for free and we were both there, he pointed at Ge and himself. He was introduced in Chinese for this unscheduled recital by the Austrian ambassador. Go ask him. His opening Bach suite received such a thunderous ovation it brought tears to his wife. Mr. Kriesler then repeated the Bach before going on with his program, and later repeating the Beethoven sonata as well for a solo recital that went on for longer than two hours without intermission all before his scheduled evening concert with the SMO.

Sure that *Deutschland über alles* could not understand Xian's Cantonese, Ge translated it for him, even though he did not know any more beyond the four words *diu nei lou mou*. Mr. Xian said it's always dangerous to use music for political purposes, and you should be cautious coming from a country steeped in the religious and political confrontations over music between the Lutherans, Catholics and Johann Sebastian.

After a pause Ge added, Yes, he said all that and more, It could come back and bite you, or for that matter end up encouraging the production and performance of bad marching music.

25

Over the next week, Xian and Ge exchanged several emails about going to Hong Kong together to meet with their friend PK Leung and to check out the post-colonial music scene, but Xian had to cancel at the last moment as he had just worked out the instrument and choral mixes for his major composition he had been working on to complete. So the first thing Ge said to PK when they met on the second floor of the Drunken Boat Restaurant on Hennessy in Wan Chai, Xian is almost finished with the *Yellow River Cantata* with full chorus and Chinese ethnic music instruments.

It's quite amazing how he's used those instruments, PK said in the English that they both understood and started into the crispy eel sizzled in hot oil with chili slivers and preserved young ginger. The erhu, dahu, sanxian, bamboo flute and especially the minor-keyed harmonica. Someone'll probably have to rescore it for western orchestras.

Here's to those musicians who dare muck with the original score, Ge toasted from the bottle of Johnnie Walker Red he had picked up a block away.

And to translators, PK added, especially those older ones north of here who seem to have learned their English from the Russians or American Southern Baptists from Texas or South Carolina.

This shelter crab with black beans and garlic seems to have something else in it. Ge licked some more of the juices on a crab leg and asked, You know this?

Yes, chili, like that mantis prawn with sea salt and chili with lime added. I think the chef got that idea from Vietnamese or Shanghai cooking. We have a Cantonese saying, *doi zyu sin*, a pragmatic pocketing of what you've got. Like the umbrella protests against Beijing vetting the candidates for the upcoming CEO election, a titular position with no authority over the 70-member freely elected Legislative Council. You know Hong Kong has long been an island of rumor mongers beginning back in the days when there was a Colonial Office in London, and today's international media perpetuates that muck. Especially the American journalists exploiting the 25th anniversary of the T^2 crackdown coming up in two days. As if they don't know anything else in China or Hong Kong to write about, which they know their home readers don't give a shit about anyway but continue to feign ignorance.

Here's one for you—maybe they should write about that? But no, I hear that on the day of the anniversary, Oxford University Press will be launching a new book by this Chinese-British writer who used to string for the BBC. *The People's Republic of Amnesia: Tiananmen Revisited.*

Actually not a bad title without the colonitis, PK interrupted.

Another candlelight vigil on the tennis courts in Victoria Park for the Hong Kong people to remember T^2 and bash China? Ge picked up his Scotch and added, These Chinese wannabe writers profiteering by writing for the foreign media especially with active evangelical support, always bashing the government's crackdown in T^2 and its subsequent amnesia and human rights violations. Of course what happened in 1989 is criminal and should be remembered and those responsible held accountable, but there're other things that are news in China. No wonder foreigners know next to nothing about China or Hong Kong. Even the Hong Kong people pretend that the Brits had never screwed them over in its cultural domination and apartheid occupational policies since it was ceded to them in 1841, 1842, 1860, and again in 1898 and ruled by an appointed governor with absolute authority over the colony. Hong Kongers weren't even allowed to vote until it was returned to China in 1997.

Maybe that's enough. You didn't come all this way from Shanghai just to rant about the American news media. Movies? Have you seen Tarantino's new movie *Django Unchained*, like Tara revisited in *Gone with the Wind*, another American southern history lesson.

You're a funny guy PK.

The first one, the epic *Gone with the Wind* could have been made in Hengdian's 8,000 acre studios, just like the serials they are currently producing as history lessons for Chinese television. As you known, under the tight control of the State Administration of Radio, Film and Television, their movies must avoid controversy and contemporary topics. Betrayals and double crossings are okay, but they've also banned travelling back in time, casually made-up myths with monstrous and weird plots, and the promotion of feudalism, superstition, talismans and especially reincarnation.

Doesn't that just about take care of everything, Ge asked, like both *Gone with the Wind* and *Django Unchained?* No wonder so many movie-makers come down to Hong Kong to make their movies. Here's raising my glass to that.

Add my glass to the Americans, who have it beat easily, with their melodramatic and happy endings to contribute to their four hundred daily lies, like the knight on white horse rescuing the delinquent princess in *Pretty Woman.* And they don't even have a state agency to mandate it—it's these self-serving and self-perpetuating voluntary cons that epoxy them together as a country, north and south, east and west. This is self-censorship at its debilitating worst, prior restraint below consciousness.

To tonight then, PK added and translated one of his oral Cantonese poems composed on the spot:

Tonight then, against pockets of crowding and breathless,
he makes it to the simplicity of tea and home
for the moment. But his neighbors call him ancient,
so he emigrates to the north or south, east or west,
where he memorizes the new laws and adopts a new language
to meet the new faces everyday
and abandons the cage of his old cynicism.

They both paused for a moment before PK added, Sometimes it just doesn't come out right, and started laughing so loud the manager came over to their table and asked, What's so funny?

And one of them said, The politicians are arguing for us to be quiet and stop laughing so they can decide which one of them we will vote for, before filling their glasses again.

26

News of the barefoot lawyer's arrest went viral all over the Internet. On a whim Ge and Mr. Bogotá *Páshǒu* decided to attend Sunday's service for foreigners with passports or resident permits at the Community Church on Hengshan Lu to hear what the resident Chinese minister would have to say about the incident that was attracting international attention, especially the evangelical team in Midland, Texas, Ge learned when his PandaPow VPN jumped the wall onto Dr. Google.

Americans love the Chinese, the minister began the sermon in English, echoed in almost perfect Mandarin for a Southern Baptist from Midland, Bogotá Man pointed to the visiting preacher's biographical description in the Sunday bulletin, and cupped his hand and whispered, but why the long face and the melancholic tone?

At this point Ge started taking notes in his notebook, convinced he could interest Mr. Editor to publish a piece on the role that American missionaries have played in the cultural and political relations between the two countries, focusing on that self-taught lawyer from Shandong

Province: as long as they are either Christians or political defectors, or both, with extra credit if they are against abortion, gun control or gay marriage. It's a twisted syllogism: your enemy is my enemy; therefore you are my friend.

When it came out in the following weekend's magazine section, the lead paragraph was followed by That much we already know, but add to this delusional deductive reasoning another predicate: Midland, Texas, home of George W. Bush, a lot of Texas oil and gas dollars and champion high school football teams, and home to a Bob Fu, a defected Chinese converted by American fundamentalist Christians passing themselves off as foreign experts teaching conversational English at Liaochang Teachers College, and later a self-ordained pastor of yet another separatist evangelical sect replete with bible schools, before becoming the designated travel agent of evangelized Chinese Christians seeking passage to the United States.

Bogotá Man pulled on Ge's notebook and asked what he was doing.

Shhhhhh, Ge silenced him and went back to his notes which later turned into:

He's not a Missouri Synod Lutheran or Southern Baptist which did not renounce its racist positions until less than twenty years ago, but he fits right into the middle of the two-hundred year love-hate romance between American missionaries and the Heathen Chinee, a name used by Bret Harte in a parody (ègǎo), but like the use of metaphor (yǐnyǔ), parable (bǐyù), allegory (yùyàn), or aphorism (jìngjù) that's filled with booby traps full of fearless tigers—that delicate but dangerous and ambiguous line between them— it backfired.

These Christian references were becoming familiar to Ge, after spending most of last week digging into their histories, beginning with the first separatist Martin Luther's lengthy proclamation of independence, the ninety-five theses sent to the Vatican on the Internet as a PDF early in the 16th century, and the secession of the Southern Baptist because of its pro-slavery position in the 19th century. Particularly revealing were some documents he read which described Luther as a functional illiterate who somehow managed to write fifty-five thick volumes of tyrannical, anti-Semitic, epiphanous and indulgent tracts that passed for sermons, catechisms, and other prophetic discoveries.

Next Ge described the blind, self-taught barefoot lawyer Chen Guangcheng's confrontations over reproductive and property tax issues with the local constabulary and corrupt judiciary structure of his rural Dongshigu, who became a spontaneous international human rights *cause célèbre*, attracting the attention of the American Embassy in Beijing and the Law School at New York University, as well as a prime candidate championed by the American evangelical Christian organizations still obsessed with converting the Heathen Chinee, and the Midland Texas travel agency of pastor Bob Fu, the China Aid Association. Journalists from the BBC, Hong Kong media, and the United States print, Internet, and the endless talkheads on their 24/7 radio and television programs, initiated calls for his nomination for a Nobel Peace Prize. In the long tradition of the missionary–kid Henry Luce legacy with his arsenal of publications, *Time* magazine inserted his name to its annual list of 100 men and women whose moral examples have transformed the world.

Don't forget the backstory, Bogotá Man reminded Ge when they crossed the Avenue Pètain to the bowling alley. Beginning in the middle of the 19th century, these Methodists, Presbyterians after their failed Spalding mission with the Nez Perce in Idaho, LCMS+ULCA+NLM, SAC, CCC, YIC, Southern Baptists, Mormons, Pentecostals, and others more fundamental, came to China as missionaries—avenging angels set loose among the scold of Heathen Chinee and other Celestials—and went home rife with their personal experiences to enlighten their congregations, stealing babies and antique elm or rosewood furniture along the way, conflating missionary with mercenary.

They are accepted as trusted China experts and gracious speakers who make the luncheon circuit at the Kiwanis, Rotary, Chamber of Commerce, and assorted animal lodges such as the Moose, Elks, Lions, Eagles. Many of them will be interviewed by journalists for their regional newspapers' weekend editions. Some will write their good earth memoirs and talk about the evils of China's one-child policy, while ignoring that there's a lower percentage of children in China who go to bed at night hungry than in the United States and a huge swath of regions that have a voluntary negative birth rate.

The last thing I found out about him, Ge raised a glass of beer to his friend, this barefoot lawyer was in residence at the anti-abortion, anti-gay marriage Minuteman Institute in New Jersey, and was writing his memoir to be published by Holt (to be released) in 2015, but which can be preordered from Amazon. He was also scheduled to attend Hong Kong's opening of its June 4th Museum on Austin and Nathan, and to give a live interview with the American Enterprise Institute on the 25th anniversary of T^2.

The weekend article was accompanied by two sidebars:

It has become a tradition of American political leaders visiting China to include a pilgrimage to one of these Protestant churches, as President George W. Bush did in November of 2005 to the Gang-washi Presbyterian Church in Beijing, preceded by Secretary of State Condo-leezza Rice—daughter of a Presbyterian minister—who attended a service at the same church on the Palm Sunday in March of the same year, during which she also met with some of China's Olympic skat-ers. Three years later thousands of paid and volunteer Southern Baptists worked the crowd at the Beijing Olympics, defying the official evangelism ban. And a Texas Oral Roberts University recruitment statement for Americans to come to China disguised as teachers— *Journey to the ancient land where the national religion is Atheism and the Official color is Red. You will preach the Gospel to orphans who are bombarded with the lies of Communism and challenge college students to seek the truth of scripture in their universities. Teach English to college-age students and share the Lord while you share your language.*

Followed by a second one from the Lutheran Church Missouri Synod in St. Louis—*In a country like China, English teachers enjoy special status that affords them the opportunity to share their world-view in ways that others can't. Even though missionaries in the traditional sense can not be placed here, Christian teachers can. Moreover, schools often welcome Christian teachers as they find them hard working, compassionate,*

ALEX KUO

honest and trustworthy. These teach-
ers function in a dual role as ambas-
sadors of the faith as well as ambas-
sadors of the West. While they work to
teach and build relationships with stu-
dents and co-workers at their schools,
these teachers enjoy a wonderful rela-
tionship with college staff and officials.

After reading the piece in the paper the following weekend, Bogotá Man texted Ge: *we been fucked. They picked our pockets clean.*

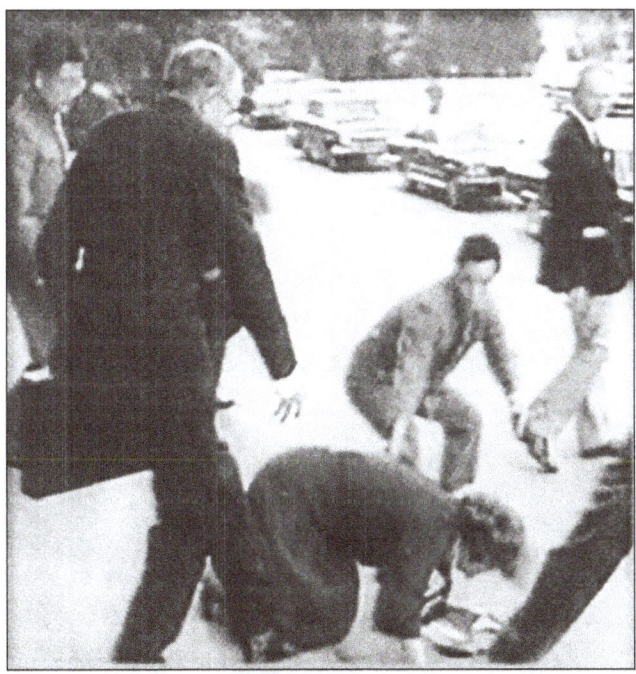

PHOTO CREDIT: Xinhua News Agency, 1982

On top of that PK sent him a smart phone image taken at the June 4th Museum at the west end of Austin Road, a collage of random objects picked up from T², including several KFC Picnic Buckets crushed under the weight of the PLA's main battle tanks, a torn *Sound of Music* t-shirt, a worn copy of Jane Austen's *Pride and Prejudice,* a Frisbee, a replica of Margaret Thatcher's handbag which she dropped when she tripped on the front steps of the Great Hall of the People during her 1982 state visit to T^2, a Hello Kitty bookbag, a flattened pull-tab can of Coke, and a life-size mannequin of Princess Di dressed as Wonder Woman in a blue miniskirt with white stars, kinky knee-high red boots, with a Medal of Freedom hanging between her taut tits.

Somehow these two messages did not get blocked by Dai Li's Lenovo firewalls, and will surely lead to Ge getting picked up for an enhanced interrogation.

27

For his continuing series on the current music calendar, Ge interviewed the Shanghai Symphony Orchestra music director Maestro Zhang Jiemin about the planning of the program for the upcoming Shanghai Spring Music Festival sponsored by the German Consulate, Nieer Piano, Siemens, Lenovo, and Mercedes-Benz of Shanghai. One of his questions was directed at recruiting voice students from the Conservatory to fill out the chorus for the Bach Coffee Cantata 211 included in the program.

Much better than those Lutheran choirs. Bach didn't think they could sing or read music, she winced and shook her hair. Much better. Those amateur hand-holding 18th century singers fucked up his music so bad he decided to write his B minor Mass and other major choral pieces for the better singers at the Catholic church across the street. He wanted to get away from the Lutheran music-ed schools with their classes for students juggling yogurt containers filled with stones, and spent what spare time he had with university singers at coffee houses and bars.

Ei! Wie schmeckt der Kaffee süße, she sang and lightly conducted the coffee aria with her fingers open while dodging Ge's photographer's camera at the same time.

Ge had seen her conduct this way before, but he wanted her to talk about it for his interview. You never seem to close your fingers when you're at the podium, can you talk about that?

Of course, of course. I never use fists or elbows, not even for the Russian heavies, the Shostakovich Seventh or Tchaikovsky 1812. Not like Mahler. Hitler admired his style, and imitated his movements for his own thunderous speeches.

You are doing a Mozart symphony, the Ninth, and the rumor circulating the Bund is that the German naval attaché is furious at you for rescoring it for this festival, no?

Ah yes, I see now this is what the interview is all about, isn't it, she smiled. Rescoring is always a challenge. The cellists I know, they all insist on rescoring Haydn's *B-flat Major String Trio Divertimento* by deleting, she emphasized with an index finger erasure, deleting the complete first movement, or they won't play it at all. Xian Xinghai's *Yellow River Cantata* has been rescored a number of times, including one that turned it into a piano concerto from the original choral piece—and it wasn't for Lang Lang—she interrupted herself and pointed a caution. In a few instances the prologue or the third movement has been omitted. And of course pianists will not perform Mozart's D major *Coronation* concerto for which he had forgotten to write the left hand part of the entire *Larghetto* second movement, unless they're willing to write it themselves or steal someone else's work, like maybe Serkin's.

This doesn't include those amateur orchestras that omit entire movements because they don't have the talent to play them, Ge interrupted.

Yes, so what's the big deal?

And off the record, she pointed again, that German *Korvettenkaptiän* doesn't know anything about music beyond drinking songs and band music, something he can thump his marching boots to, German or not. Having lived in Berlin when I was a student at the Universität der Künste, I am convinced most Germans won't even bother to cross the street to listen to a free recital. I'm also convinced they never really wanted to be Germans—they would have liked to be gypsies or Slavs or French, but little Wolfie really wanted to be German and gave them a reason to want to be German. So what's the big deal in rescoring the Mozart Ninth? Bet you his only familiarity with Mozart at home was Mozart Balls or Mozart Bonbons—Die Echte Reber Mozart-kugel wrapped in gold foil. So why does he give a shit, except his *Deutschland über alles* mentality just won't allow any Chinese to muck around with a German score. A pity, a pity.

Back on the record then, what are you thinking about rescoring in the Ninth?

Well, I don't know yet exactly. It's not an aggressive piece in C major. Its tempi should be confident but not arrogant, showy or loud. It is somewhat intelligent. I don't want the *Andante* second to linger, maybe omit its many repeats, too much redundancy for a slow movement. Maybe interchanging oboe and trombone parts in the opening *Allegro*. All together cutting it from its crowd pleasing eleven minutes of silly musical entertainment to a tolerable nine.

As you can tell, she added with a smile, I've never been able to get too excited about any of Mozart's symphonic music. Eleven is way too long. Same with his keyboard writing, and I say this as a soloist who's recorded several of his piano sonatas and concertos. A few beautiful lyrical passages here and there in the middle movements, but for the most part pretty boring stuff. Some days I find everything in Mozart can stand some editing. But his opera work now, she interrupted herself and repeated, his opera work now, that's a different tune altogether, she laughed, ready for the camera.

As they were leaving her studio after the end of the interview, she stopped them and asked, Hey dudes, why did the chicken stop crossing the road?

The photographer set down his equipment bags and tripod, raised his right hand and answered, Because it was chicken?

Ge added, Because it was tired?

No, no, Maestro Zhang wagged a finger. Because it was tired of all the chicken jokes.

28

Ge was having his doubts about his work, both his public writing as a journalist and culture writer for his newspaper with its international syndications, and his fiction that's not been seeing much print, not commercially viable, Mr. Editor had said a number of times. Ge had just run into a recent Beijing translation of an essay by the American writer Simon Ortiz and was drawn to his statement, "If it's fiction, you better believe it," at a time when he has become increasingly convinced that journalism at its best is only a narcotic used to reassure the middle class that everything in their world is okay and that they can continue to go shopping, as he had said to Kuifang at the Old Station last week. A lie is a lie, is a lie, is a lie, he repeated to himself.

He thought China had very few serious authors writing at the moment or at least getting published, and fewer yet who were reading their work, especially at a time when there was a great need for it. The wars against the Japanese and against each other, two centuries of foreign occupation and exploitation, sanctions, children suffering, tuberculosis, small pox, hepatitis A & B, gonorrhea, cholera, typhoid, malaria, dysentery, famine from both drought and flood, and just plain impoverishment and exhaustion, led to the impossibility of developing an effective indigenous government short of a total and devastating revolution. The combination of these realities was asking his fiction to step aside.

Perhaps it's just humanly impossible to rise above the patriotic fervor of the moment and write something intelligent and perceptive about it, non-fiction or fiction. Maybe it'll just have to wait until that later tranquil moment before one can write truthfully about it, as in what really happened in T^2 in 1989 and why, or in Ortiz's case, Wounded Knee in South Dakota in 1973. These writers today were quick to hit the delete button to obliterate an entire dynasty they don't like and then flee south, changing their name every week. The T^2 story told by insiders and outsiders was full of incriminations, apologetics, revenge or outright lies appropriated for personal aggrandizement or collective memorialization or both, or just plain forgotten and ignored, too complex to think through, better to drop it and move on and not look up from our smart phones or iPads.

In Ge's world new ideas were never discussed by either the party apparatchik or university intellectuals publicly or privately, but their soft and compromised versions were circulating in diluted form, plagiarized and re-circulated in article after article, book after book, year after year, while the economic and cultural gaps between the rich and the poor were stretched to its widest limits in China's long history of inherited and corrupted mercantile wealth. He read that Lu Xun had said it was time for China to stop telling lies about itself and start looking at the other side of the moon. He made that statement close to a century ago, and nothing much has changed since then.

Its people still have no understanding of who they are, whose history has been kidnapped from them and replaced with the march of empty nationalism repeated a hundred times a day and schooled in a book of a thousand lies until it has no meaning to anyone at all. Ideas were quickly borrowed, or pirated and branded before its own industrious and talented workforce was outsourced to foreign shores, everything merging into one indistinguishable amorphous blog that no one read until it was too late, not even the watchdogs in the Ministry of Intellectual Purity with their latest Israel Ibit Peregrine surveillance technology, eliminating the last meridian of hope, bogged down by the long history of refusal to publicly critique the stale and harmonious perceptions of the self and state, except for the short-lived student demonstrations in 1900, 1912, 1919, 1928, 1966, and again in 1989, these repetitions necessitated because the earlier barricades hadn't changed a thing, not a thing, except that during those historical convulsions people's lives go through their own revolutions, wanted or not, sometimes for the better, sometimes for the worse, with no choice whatsoever.

Maybe Kuifang was right, again, I'm becoming too much of a moralist and a bore to be a writer of any kind. I'll just look at this period as an intermission, time for a break and think about taking up something new, like bungee jumping, or learning to play bridge.

29

But before that was to happen, Ge was sidetracked by a story told to him by a beggar on the WeiHai Lu shortcut Ge was taking around the museum to get to his office.

He guessed the beggar looked older than he was, and appeared to be wearing the same but recently washed clothes he had on in Jiangwan two years ago when the Japanese naval bombardment totally annihilated this district to the northeast of Shanghai. One of his dark hands was holding on to a child with him, maybe a three year old girl, and the other was open and asking. It was the gentle expression in his eyes that separated him from a sea of beggars that made Ge stop and give all the money he had on him, even when he suspected the man may have hired the little girl for prop and prosperity.

Xiè xiè, xiè xiè.

He then put a hand on Ge's arm and said in the same halting Mandarin of the Uighur woman's, I have story for you, and pointed in the direction of the museum two blocks away.

The three of them leaned against the building and slowly sat down. The man put the money into a pocket and brought out a handkerchief-wrapped round object and carefully with both hands untied the knot and gave the roasted sweet potato to the little girl between them before beginning his story.

See museum there, he pointed again, strange story. I work there before Japanese came. In basement, how do you say in English, *Xīnshēng dài* research.

Cenozoic, I think, Ge interrupted and brought out his notebook. He was not going to miss this one.

Peking Man, complete *tóugǔ*, head, no, no, yes, cranium, cranium, full cranium, no damage, no decay, nearly *bǎi wàn* years old. Then, as if his limited Mandarin would short circuit his description to a foreigner, he paused and resorted to a metaphor, as if that would clarify everything, and get into an American fortune cookie, Ge added in his notes, looking over at the little girl enjoying the sweet potato, savoring it ever so slowly and not dropping a single crumb.

Looked thoughtful and melancholy alone in basement, he continued, even when goon from gangster Dai Li's Investigation and Statistics Bureau came with new Document Six, cannot talk it, cannot write it, those gaps in human history. Most important, hide from Japanese. For safe keeping until war all over, send cranium with American Marines to New York, American Museum Natural History, Franz Boas. Japanese no steal, no destroy.

Ge stopped his note taking, examined the man, but he looked truthful enough. How could he make up such a story, Ge asked himself. The beggar next described taking a course in the history of archaeology in China at Fudan thirty years later, where the professor delivered a slightly different variation of this story.

Are you sure about this, Ge asked.

Yes. I worked there before. The cranium is not there now. You go see no.

The professor's lecture placed the skull found in a cave just outside Beijing on Dragon Bone Hill, *Zhōukǒudiàn*, and stored it in a basement closet in the embryonic Cenozoic Research Institute of the Peking Union Medical College. The Imperial Japanese Army confiscated the skull sometime between 1937 and 1940, and sent it to Nanjing before deciding to transfer it across the Black Ditch to its secure Imperial Japanese Navy base in Keelung, Taiwan, sometime in 1944, before shipping it to Yokohama. But an American submarine torpedoed and sank the cargo ship from Keelung, and the 800 centuries old skull went down with it.

What we have then, Ge scribbled in his notes, are two variations of history, both without evidence. Such is the messiness of history; it's no wonder historians don't want the truth.

He looked over at the man who had just finished telling his story and was beginning to get up. He appeared relieved and younger, thoughtful and a little melancholic, like his description of the Peking Man. The girl, who had finished the sweet potato by now, got up and smiled at Ge for the first time.

It was Ge's turn to thank, *xiè xiè*, and had whispered to himself that before, but.

30

All was not going well for the tour guide with her wards wandering off in all directions, a scold of malingerers not sure of what they're looking at—hairpins that would challenge a Transportation Security Agency security scan, glass vials with painted rose petals, some with a certificate authenticating the dust of a Mongolian tiger's mandible, rear-view mirror animal talismans, stacks of calligraphic sketches of rural domestic flora and fauna, and the two most expensive items, the history-impaired Zippo lighters hand-engraved with P-40 Warhawks or *Flying Tygers*, and little red books in Chinese which the tourists were not sure if they were Mao instructions for making plastic explosives in one's kitchen, or a Latter-Day Saints abbreviated translation of the New Testament—global flotsam leftover from the last pirate days flea market [last seen littered across the battlefield of the Little Big Horn that even the Arapaho, Lakota and Northern Cheyenne women did not pick up to trade at their gatherings], and everything oh so cheap in real money. Some stopped to pick up a few fake Mao memorabilia or PLA souvenirs, snap a dozen digitals

PHOTO CREDIT: Zoe Filipkowska

of the trained and chained ospreys [cormorants] diving for bottom fish in the canal by the bridge, an old man in a fancy dark mohair blazer playing miniature bumper pool by himself, a cigarette in his mouth, like Minnesota Fats in a remote Witness Protection Program. She blew her whistle barely heard above the din, but no one paid any attention to the fluttering rescue-orange banner over her head.

Looks like an American group, Kuifang said to Ge, shaking her head. Not Germans; they would stay together, not wander away. Australians maybe. Very vulgar, very loud.

Ge was beginning to regret accompanying her to this early Ming Dynasty canal village of Tongli where she wanted to find out more about its famous peanut, sesame and walnut Wansan cakes and rice balls. Even though it was only mid-morning in the middle of the week, the tourists were arriving in such numbers and turning the narrow streets into the chaos of a thousand carnivals, even the local dogs were tucking in their tails and crawling back into the safety of their homes. But it was still good to get away from the pollution and heat of the city, a fast train ride, and besides, there could be material here for either his public writing or his fiction, or both, he thought, getting out his notebook.

They're Americans, Ge said to Kuifang. You can tell, they're all over-weight, and retired men wearing white tube socks inside their Birkenstocks.

One of them and his wife were putting on the colorful native costumes for a photo documenting their reaching out to the resident ethnic minority group.

Just like we did outside Chengdu with the Miao last week, she said, prancing around in their elaborately embroidered gowns, [as if she's in a hoop dance she had pilfered from a Pine Ridge Reservation pow wow in South Dakota where she last vacationed].

To complete the cross-cultural appreciation experience, this couple stepped into a gilded litter [jiǎn yú] and on the wobbling shoulders of two porters, crossed the round-arched Taiping Bridge, masquerading their way to their wedding for good luck, or banished 3,000 miles west to Kazakhstan by the imperial magistrate who had found them wanting.

PHOTO CREDIT: Zoe Filipkowska

By now the Birkenstocked husband had had enough. What's the big deal, he barked at one of the porters without looking at him, but certain he could not understand English. Venice was much better, he said louder this second time so the guide could hear. At least we didn't have to look at their laundry hanging out to dry, and pointed an accusing finger at the nearest alley cluttered with rows of family washing.

At least it's much easier now, they're only words of an ugly tourist, Ge started writing in his notebook. Yesterday there were laws. In addition to the occupying Japanese, too many laws of too many expanding countries to remember— the Russian, the French, the British, China Charlton Heston Gordon with his American Marines, and of course Dai Li's unscripted commandments, an umbrella gripped in the fists of imperial and extra territoriality covering all of Shanghai in a country whose last reigning emper- or Puyi abdicated in 1912 with the help of the Japanese near the final stages of the sloven Qing Dynasty, and the country was then stuck with it for the next thirty years, rain or shine. Even though they were words, they are what we use to connect with each other. What was he really expecting when he bought his ticket to come over here with his wife, and why doesn't he keep his constant dissing to himself.

I see what you're writing down, Kuifang leaned over and interrupted. Maybe you should give that guide over there your script. She was giving her patrons a blowjob with her megaphone, an itchy intimacy promoting a fantasy culture that they'll take home as cherished memories of China. It's a good thing the locals don't understand English.

After a loud splash, the crowd leaned toward the walled embankment near the bridge where a tourist had slipped into the canal.

Àodàlìyǎ, yóu yǒng, yóu yǒng, fān kuei, the crowd was yelling.

What're they saying, Ge asked.

They think he's Australian, foreign ghost, and they're asking him to swim.

On the thirty-minute train ride back to Hongqiao Station, Ge looked past Kuifang across the aisle at an older man dressed in a dated workman blue cotton suit who had removed his glasses and was using them as a magnifying glass, first on the print of a right-hand page of the paperback he had been reading, then the cover of the book, then the latticed epidermis of his left hand, then finally on the small tear in the seat in front of him, whereupon Ge copied this live feed right into his notebook, where I do not wring my hands and rend my clothes over senseless crimes, violence over living things, disasters and corporate malfeasance, and I am not the connoisseur of certainty and stability and harmony, but I will bring those stories to you that I believe are important for us to remember.

31

Give up or things will get worse, the mean, local Beijing *Gōng 'ānjú* [Public Security] officer warned me, and threatened me with twenty years of imprisonment in their notorious Qincheng Prison Number 156, one year for each one of the twenty paintings I had vandalized. But I was lucky. The serious State Security people took over the interrogation. They sent me here instead.

Ge was on another assignment in Beijing, this time to interview the award-winning painter Bi Xiewie detained in the HuiLongGuan psychiatric hospital in the quiet Changping District northwest of the city. Under orders from the State Security Bureau for psychological evaluation. The intake diagnosis Ge was allowed to see listed ten possible explanations for Bi's unusual behavior: 1) work-related stress; 2) bi-polar personality; 3) chose wrong profession; 4) autism; 5) dissociative amnesia; 6) early stages of Alzheimer's; 7) attention deficit disorder; 8) bad work habits; 9) drinks too much tea, 10) drinks too much alcohol; 11) does not drink enough alcohol, and 12) voted for the wrong candidate.

How did you get this coveted appointment in the first place?

A few years back when I was about to graduate from the Central Academy of Art with a M.F.A. and no job prospect in sight, I responded to a Draw Me contest in a matchbook and submitted it. It was a downsized sketch of a squirrel, Mr. Bi said, and my copy was quite good, actually.

Six months later I was thrilled when two suits trotted to his apartment from their polished black Hongqi to inform him that he had won. What had I won? I had forgotten the squirrel completely, and was drinking too much bitter melon beer that day. They whisked me off to T^2 and down to a dimly lit painter's workshop in the basement below the Tiananmen Gate. I had won the contest to be the country's artist laureate tenured for life that included an enviable allowance for lodging and food in addition to the handsome monthly spending money. From more than 200,000 entries, mind you, he said, which explained why the jury and the Minister of Culture took six months to adjudicate.

It turned out my job was to paint Chairman Mao Zedong's portrait to hang on top of the Tiananmen Gate to Heavenly Peace, replacing Chiang Kaishek's. It was great, and I felt honored for the appointment. I had complete freedom to order the best materials, canvas from Kunming, acrylic paints from Winsor and Newton, French sable brushes, rosewood frames from the Philippines. Nothing but the best. A dream job. I even got to meet

PHOTO CREDIT: Peter Griffin

ALEX KUO

the Chairman a couple of times, but both times he was quite distracted by the two teenage girls stroking the bulge in his lap. But Premier Zhou Enlai's office was very helpful and provided me with hundreds of close up photographic images for my work.

A very celebratory official ceremony accompanied the installation of the thirty feet by twenty open painting over the Gate, and Mr. Chairman shook my hand and graciously thanked me for my work. Just about everyone from the Most Central Committee was present for this occasion, some in wheelchairs, some on crutches, along with cameras from all the major media networks in the country.

All well and good. Tourists from inside and outside China took millions of photographs of Mao's portrait at this popular site on every travel agent's agenda, and I had lots of free time to leisurely stroll around the square with my VIP pass to every site and event, including the Imperial Palace.

Then it began to rain. And it snowed. And it rained, he repeated, waving his arms up and down. The portrait and the canvas had both been treated, and at first they stood up under the changing weather. But after a month, it was decided that the painting had to be replaced. Once more then, into the paint shop, a second portrait, an exact replica of the first, from memory.

Then in the second year, another, and another after another, even after the death of the Chairman in 1976 after his meeting with American President Richard Nixon.

First I tried to amuse myself by painting the Chairman slightly differently from one portrait to the next, his hairline receding just a bit more, or a little less, eyes slightly crossed, or looking to the west or the east, the collar on his tunic sometimes unbuttoned, sometimes looking a little grim, sometimes with a slight smile, a little monkey wrench here and there just to entertain myself.

With this kind of repetitive work, I was becoming disenchanted with this appointment. The invigorating conversations I had been having with visitors to the square and the palace were beginning to turn to the trivial and the mundane. The students and the intellectuals who used to paste their dissident views in big character posters on the walls of the square were losing their interest in politics, no ideological bent within the runaway economy that seemed to position them into an ever expanding middle class, that shelter which widens the buffer that protects the privileged rich from the threat of the oppressed victims on whose backs they prosper. They were more involved with their own career trajectories and how to find a cheaper apartment in Beijing.

Desperate, I took evasive action. I hid and altered my identity by knocking off a stroke in the radical of my family name to change its meaning and confound the bureaucrats, so they won't be able to find me in their dictionary. When that didn't work, I tried changing the address on all my cards, the residence card, the library card, the T^2 VIP pass, my two ATM bank cards, and crushed the memory card in my cell phone. I told my neighbors I was hitch hiking to Shanghai with Franz Kafka. But none of that worked, the PSB agents would always find me and take me back within two days.

Then one night I just could not take it any longer and got drunk with some artist friends at a pub near the academy. With perhaps too much Maotai to drink, we concocted a plan to scale the Tiananmen Gate and vandalize the new portrait of Chairman Mao looking to the east I had hung just a week ago in preparation for the October 1 founding day celebrations. But by the time we got there, my friends had sobered up enough to scuttle away and left me alone and half way up the ramparts with a gallon of black acrylic paint in one hand. There was nothing left for me to do but complete scaling the wall by myself and dumping the entire gallon onto this portrait, covering the Chairman completely, including what was left of his hair, and the nineteen replacement portraits leaning nearby.

By this time the smart looking uniformed and armed police had followed me up the wall, saw what I had done, cuffed me and marched me to the basement of their Ministry of Public Security national headquarters just two blocks east of the People's Heroes Monument. There I was ID-ed, booked, fingerprinted, and charged with violating multiple laws and covenants that included crimes against the people's republic, disrespectful of and defacing a national monument, insulting our most esteemed supreme leader whose mausoleum was only within a stone's throw of his portrait, disturbing the harmony of the community, creating a bad image of the artist and projecting an undesirable role model for budding artists, polluting the environment with the spilled paint, wasting public monies, and disturbing the peace and fomenting dissent.

After six hours of intense and threatening interrogation by the rotating local Public Security team, fortunately the State Security representatives claimed extra-territorial jurisdiction because the crimes were committed on state property and against a government artifact, and took a lighter view of what I had done and remanded me to this hospital for evaluation, observation and correction. And there you have it. I may well have been the first and last artist laureate this country will ever have.

In the cab to the South Station and back to Shanghai, Ge looked over his notes trying to decide how impossible it'll be for him to improve on Mr. Bi's own narrative of what happened to him. Just sometimes a story is told best by the person who's still living in it, and no amount of interpretation or literary embellishment can improve it and will in fact muck it up and destroy it. Ge concluded that he was lucky to have heard it first hand, and had no intention of translating it for his editor.

The train station was crammed with people. Both Ge and his editor had forgotten this was the first week in May, the time for the annual meeting of the National People's Congress and its 2,987 delegates, plus the representatives from Hong Kong, Macau and Taiwan, and all their families and middle school history teachers, along for their annual pilgrimage to the capitol's sights as well as the Great Wall, and they're coming on the speed train and the slow train, from Lhasa, Chengdu, Guangzhou, Chongqing, Lanzhou, Ulan Bator, Heilongjiang, Hohhot, everywhere on the continent that is China and wannabe, or not China and don't wannabe, all of them travelling on the government's machine-printed yuan, embellished with the portrait of a smiling Chairman Mao in brown.

32

Ge started his talk by saying that even without taking into account the concept of reincarnation that will take care of itself in the Möbius strip, the further we followed a sequence of events into the past, the more a random and seemingly trivial event could easily lead to a complex and almost infinite set of consequences. For example, he said off the cuff and without notes, had the Peking Man been careful in collecting and storing the large ostrich eggs as he had been told by the women in his family, he and his girl friend might have survived the late Pleistocene extinction event and the China we know today would not include the doomed love story of the butterfly lovers etched into our ethnic DNA.

Fudan University's film studies graduating students had asked him to give its commencement address on the topic of foreign independent films. Honored by this invitation, Ge said he would like to talk about the films of the American Quentin Tarantino and Korean Kim Ki-duk and their aesthetics of violence, provided the dean would not object to this discussion that would skirt the boundaries of the State Administration of Press, Publication, Radio, Film and Television's (PPRFT) Clause 16 which prohibits public discussion of subjects that provoke trouble in society, and bans violent content in art and entertainment.

PHOTO CREDIT: Zoe Filipkowska

Wanting to get a feel for his alma mater as well as beat the crowd, Ge arrived early and took a walk in the pale morning light. He stopped at the president's new house in the middle of campus that used to be called the White House, built by a Guo Renyuan for his experimental psychology laboratory back in the mid 1920s when he was president, a name Ge stole for an alias when he was an undergraduate writing for the school paper, and later his *nom de plume* for assigned newspaper articles about subjects he didn't want to be associated with.

Uncomfortable with his Peking Man example, Ge thought he could clarify it by referring to the old *The Love Eterne,* which he was sure everyone within hearing had seen, some perhaps as many as 500 times, a movie the director Ang Lee was said to be able to lip synch every word even before he had seen it because his parents had bought the four-record set with its complete soundtrack including the music and all of the dialogue and played repeatedly it in his home when he was growing up in Taiwan. Perhaps the suggestion for his *Crouching Tiger, Hidden Dragon*, Ge asked his audience that appeared to be slightly more comfortable with his talk now.

But as much as *The Love Eterne* is loved by millions of millions of people on all five continents and made piles of money, he continued, like

Gone with the Wind, it really does not reach beyond its limited entertainment value, and some critics have criticized both of them for the damage they have done to our perception of history, fostering a false sense of the 19th century American south as portrayed in *Gone with the Wind* and Mandarin Chinese life in Hangzhou before the two star-crossed lovers turned into butterflies and fluttered toward heaven, a Hong Kong happy ending to blur the pain of their tragic story.

Ge paused for a moment and looked at a well-dressed and attractive young woman seated between the university president and the chancellor in the middle of the cordoned-off reserved front row for university officials. She was not capped-and-gowned like everyone else with their black mortar boards, the hoods of their gowns and velvet sleeves emblazoned with iridescent pinks, golds, purples, and she was taking voluminous notes throughout his address as if she were a correspondent trying to get everything down right for her next bylined magazine article about a culture writer disguised as a commencement speaker giving a talk about violence in the New Wave independent films, or an undercover PPRFT agent taking incriminating notes, which is highly unlikely—but one can never be too sure about that—or a writer trying to extract the right words or phrases for the short story she was working on.

After spending a few moments on how the confusion of motives impacts the decisions one makes in life and how that ultimately affects the reincarnation possibilities in which Ge paraphrased one of Kim's guiding spirits, the modern Korean Buddhist monk Seongcheol, a butterfly may be just a butterfly in whatever life, a mountain is just a mountain, life is life, however others may disrespect it, Ge moved on to a serious discussion about the beautiful and violent study of emotional conflict at the heart of both Tarantino and Kim's films where reality and fantasy meet, how *Django Unchained* looked at the 19th century history of the American South that was left out of *Gone with the Wind,* including the violence resulting from racism and its Ku Klux Klan champions, and how Kim's *Bad Guy* explores the lives of people who matter in spite of the violence surrounding their marginalized lives.

From the way the university dignitaries lingered after their applause at the end of the address, Ge's thought they were not disturbed by his talk—Dai Li may not arrest him just yet—and appeared to be more than pleased with his discussion about violence and film, not that he cared at all. The young woman stood to the side looking at her notes and waited until almost everyone had stopped chatting with Ge before coming over and introducing herself.

Let's go off campus and get a beer, Eva said.

The neighborhood beer café just outside the university's main gate had barely been opened before Eva and Ge sat down and ordered a drink. From how she flicked her eye lashes when she introduced herself and the way she accidentally brushed against him when they were crossing against the traffic light, it was clear to Ge that she had more of an interest in him than in what he had to say about Kim or Tarantino's movies or Ge's blast against *Gone with the Wind* and *Love Eterne.*

So, how did you get to sit in the VIP front row? Are you a student here or what, Ge asked.

Growing up in western Xinjiang Province, I learned very early not to give any Han Chinese the authority to say no if I were to ask for permission. Just do it—all they can do is stop me. So she just did it, sat down before anyone had a chance to say No to her and before the officials uncomfortably squeezed in on either side of her. And yes, she was a graduating film studies student, but couldn't be bothered with the ceremonial pomp, which she saw as a fake celebration when the graduating seniors had competed with each other all year for the few scholarships and recommendations to study in Canada or the United States, especially in Vancouver or Los Angeles.

So I applied to the lower-ranked Wake Forest instead, to make sure I would get in, Eva explained.

Ge looked at Eva's hair of the Jennifer Aniston generation he identified with the popular imported television series *Friends,* and asked if she had always kept her hair at that length. You know, he continued as Eva twirled a loose strand with her right hand, you might be the last woman in Shanghai to keep her hair that long, don't you, friends or no friends.

You're asking if this shoulder grazing shag is real, now, now. We all know across the Pacific over there, she pointed in the direction of Tokyo. In Los Angeles the women have real Birkins and fake boobs, but here in Shanghai it's the other way around. Our Birkins might be fake, but not our boobs and definitely not our hair. Other things maybe, but never our hair. A wig? Damn! Besides, are you interviewing me or what?

Sorry, force of habit, he apologized, but he's actually thinking he should have known better than to be so inquisitive with a woman from that western border province, like that woman with the borrowed baby he interviewed in the Foreign Languages Bookstore two months ago. After this pause then, he asked why she was taking so many notes during his talk.

But no, she smiled and flicked her eye lashes again, I was not taking any notes. I was writing my own piece about Kim's work. Look, she opened her notebook and read from it. *Almost all of his stories unfold and explain with sensitivity and sharp observation of detail the destructive and sadomasochistic relationship between men and women in borderline social settings where pain and hope meet*, don't you think, she asked Ge at the end of that sentence.

Ge shook his head. I think you'll do well at Wake Forest.

After that the conversation appeared harmless enough and fortunately they both had to leave for their appointments, but the very next morning Ge found Eva had left a bottle of water for him on his desk at the newspaper office, and a note under it offering to go with him to another Kim or Tarantino movie or whatever before she left for her studies in North Carolina.

I'll have to put a stop to this, Ge thought. What does she want from me? Does she know what she wants? Maybe it's just my fantasy or conceit making too much of this, and there's no one else in all Shanghai she can talk with about Kim or Tarantino or Peckinpah? Maybe I can just ignore her because she's going to leave soon? No wonder there's that PPRFT Clause 16 prohibiting the public discussion of subjects that foment trouble in society. They should add a subsidiary caveat to it: don't ever muck with determined ethnic women—they'll eat you alive.

33

It was the third Friday of the month, and Kuifang and Ge were going to the Shanghai Bankers Club's monthly duplicate bridge game. As they ran to the closing door of the express elevator on the ground floor of the Bank of China Tower, Kuifang nudged Ge to be quiet. A tall woman in her thirties looked menacingly at them, irritated she had to wait for them while continuing to punch the 52 button repeatedly. Ever attentive to people's hair styles and clothing and the political statements they projected, he made mental note of her faux-layered bob cut with traditional wet pin, curl set with thin ribbons of glossy, darker blacks for a shimmering effect, as if she were waiting for the media photographers, her lip gloss matching the red of her Christian Louboutin suede pumps.

Kuifang had started patiently teaching Ge how to play the game of bridge about a year ago at the Slam Club, something they can do together maybe once a month in the new Shanghai club as well as travel to tournaments in places they wanted to visit, Harbin, Kunming, Chengdu, Hong Kong. Without a natural card sense and curiosity for numbers, Ge turned out to be a difficult student, taking him a week to memorize the basic distributional patterns of thirteen cards divided into four subsets, 4-4-3-2, 5-3-3-2, 5-4-3-1, 5-4-2-2, 4-3-3-3, 6-3-2-2 that accounted for nearly seventy-five percent of its probabilities, about all that's important for any level of the game, quite simple really, Kuifeng had tried to assure him, and that's why some of the best players are accountants or bookkeepers *ma*. All you need is to be able to add up to thirteen and then divide it into four, she explained.

She had also suggested that he read about the game, and being interested in the language of the game such as *strip squeeze, double dummy, end play,* Ge quickly devoured her extensive library on bidding systems, defense and declarer play, and the critical, competitive differences between pair and team events, even though he could not understand what he was reading most of the time. His efforts at duplicating a hand with real cards and studying their probable variations all night did not seem to help much either. He also read about the history of bridge in Shanghai and how in the 1920s

PHOTO CREDIT: Zoe Filipkowska

it was dominated by the Americans and British playing at the Shanghai Club until the American members were excluded because of their country's isolationist position in the first year of World War I. A year later in 1917 the Americans opened its own bridge club and moved with the American Chamber of Commerce and La Salle Extension University into the same building on Fuzhou Lu, an American colonial replicated by the Hungarian architect Làszlò Hudec—who had also designed the Park Hotel, Grand Theatre, Dr. Woo's Green House, the Baptist and other Christian churches—with bricks imported from the U.S. With a Charter of Incorporation, it was named the Slam Club, with membership limited to fifty-three, to correspond with the fifty-two in a deck of cards and the joker. It stayed open for seventeen years until early November of 1941 when President Roosevelt ordered the U.S. Marines to leave Shanghai because of imminent war with Imperial Japan, less than thirty days before its assault on Pearl Harbor.

Kuifang also suggested Ge read the fictional history of bridge in Shanghai, especially J.G. Ballard's *Empire of the Sun* about the twelve-year old Jim Ballard who was writing a manual on bridge by the title of *Play Contract Bridge* from

listening to his mother's bridge parties, before he had yet to play a single hand

and this author's novella "White Jade," in which two Shanghai high school girls Katherine Ling and Wu Shiung Chien played on a team seeded last against the reigning French Concession champion team the Ballards in the Grand Hotel's main ballroom and won, in a series marked by cultural contrasts, with Mrs. Ballard dressed up in a Pierrot suit and staring with steely eyes at the upshot girls

who agreed that while it is true language, the arts, and even sports and games often reflected the cultural values inherent in their origins, they can also be beautiful, challenging fun when they are disconnected from the ideological and political underpinnings. J.S. Bach's French Suites are provocative, serene, beautiful and full of possibilities, despite some people identifying them as a form of exclusive, national identity, French or German.

For now, Kuifang whispered to Ge, the woman with the shimmering hair is on Shanghai's Professional Women's Bridge Team, a corporate account executive at Dutch Shell who's been looked at for an alternate spot on the Shanghai team bound for the InterPort Tournament next month at Hainan Island's holiday resorts where the Chinese teams are paid to train for international matches. She's a predator at other player's mistakes, Kuifang warned.

But I think she's too loud to make the team, she added. She thinks her fucking Bobbi Brown high-shimmer lip gloss makes her a better player than she actually is. No one can stand to partner with her for more than a game a month.

Not paying much attention to what she was saying, Ge was more interested in looking out the 52nd floor window, a few floors above where Tom Cruise had made his bungee jump last week for the filming of MI-III, landing on the pavement on the other side of the Huangpu River almost two miles away. I guess in that kind of espionage thriller, Ge thought, this kind of mistake really doesn't matter.

About half way through the evening, Ms Bobbi Brown and her quiet partner came to Kuifang and Ge's table. Sitting North, Ge picked up a harmless looking hand, ♠-A85, ♥-8754, ♦-J764, ♣-75, about ready to pass any bid partner made, until Kuifang opened the bidding with the strong artificial 2♣ that can't be passed. After Ge's right hand opponent Ms Bobbi Brown passed, Ge made the mandatory artificial bid of 2♦, a waiting call that denied both a strong hand and a good five-card suit, just to see what kind of hand went with partner's 2♣ opening. At his turn to bid next, Ms Bobbi Brown's partner came in with a bid of 3♠, a preemptive bid telling his partner he has nothing in his hand but a lot of spades, at least six. Ge could feel a breath of exasperation from Ms Bobbi Brown to his right, her perfectly manicured fingers starting to tap the table impatiently. After a slight pause to acknowledge the skip bid of 3♠ on her right, Kuifang placed the 4NT card on the table without missing the next heart beat, as if she had expected something dramatic like that 3♠ call to come from one of her two opponents, but at the same time telling Ge she has a spade stop, and can take ten tricks on her own cards, definitely a very strong opening 2♣ bid, at least 26 high card points.

Looking at his hand, Ge liked that he also had a spade stopper, ♠-A, and his two red suits had four cards each, one of which might bring in an extra trick if the suit's remaining six cards were split 3-3 among the two opponents, and adding them to Ge's ten tricks for a total of eleven, or eleven and a squeeze of some kind for twelve, Ge bid 6NT, knowing that his partner and teacher, Ms Technician, can somehow bring home the contract.

W	N	E	S
			2♣
P	2♦	3♠	4NT
P	6NT	P	P
P			

Opening lead, ♣-J

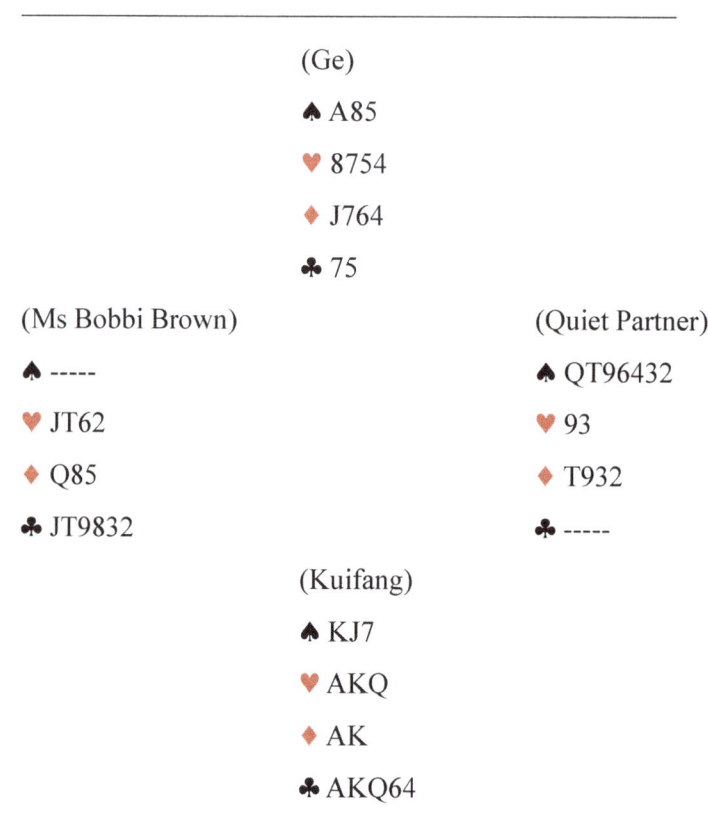

(Ge)
♠ A85
♥ 8754
♦ J764
♣ 75

(Ms Bobbi Brown)
♠ -----
♥ JT62
♦ Q85
♣ JT9832

(Quiet Partner)
♠ QT96432
♥ 93
♦ T932
♣ -----

(Kuifang)
♠ KJ7
♥ AKQ
♦ AK
♣ AKQ64

Kuifang was looking at ten tricks off the top, two in ♠, three in ♥, two in ♦, three in ♣. She will have twelve tricks finessing East for the known ♠-Q if the ♥ suit is divided three-three for a fourth ♥ trick, which is unlikely given the preemptive 3♠ bid to her right, and equally unlikely that the ♣ suit would be divided three-three for the same reason. As Ge was to learn after watching Kuifang play the hand, there was a way to take twelve tricks if Ms Bobbi Brown held four ♥s and the ♦-Q, a very likely possibility.

So on trick one Kuifang won the ♣-J lead with her ♣-A. Then she played the A, K, and Q of ♥, East showing out on the third ♠, putting four ♥s in West's hand, so far so good. Then she ran ♠-J from her hand, losing to East's ♠-Q to set up her squeeze, a move that astonished Ge, given that even he knew how to capture that ♠-Q by playing a ♠ from dummy. East returned a ♠ and Kuifeng won with her ♠-K in hand, then winning with the ♦ A and K, for a total of seven tricks and leaving the remaining distribution at

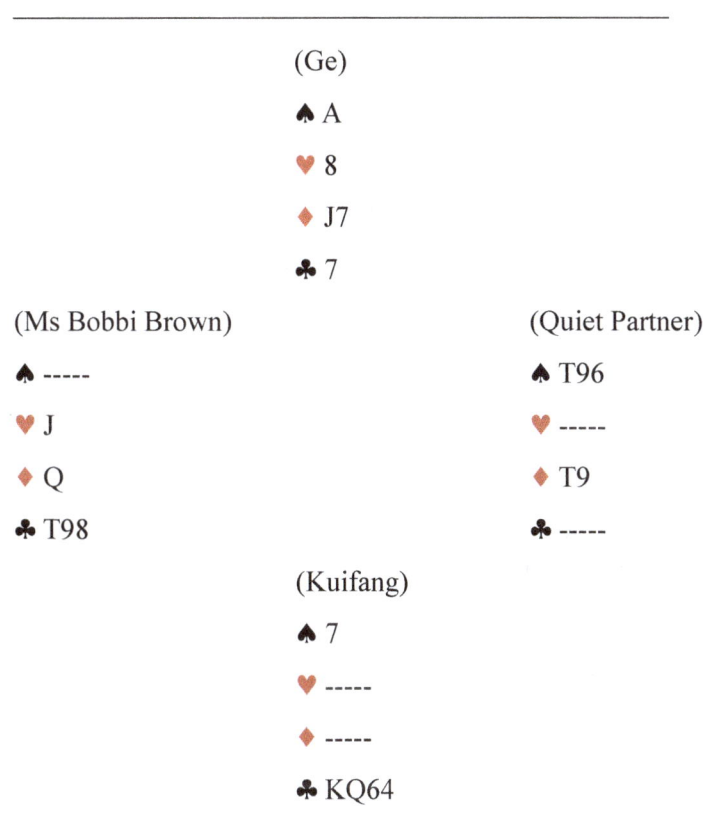

(Ge)
♠ A
♥ 8
♦ J7
♣ 7

(Ms Bobbi Brown)
♠ -----
♥ J
♦ Q
♣ T98

(Quiet Partner)
♠ T96
♥ -----
♦ T9
♣ -----

(Kuifang)
♠ 7
♥ -----
♦ -----
♣ KQ64

and she had to take all of the remaining five tricks.

Next Kuifang played the ♠-7 from her hand, and Ms Bobbi Brown, re-alizing she was fucked, started drumming the table again, louder this time. She was squeezed in three suits, triple squeezed—she could not discard a ♣ as that would allow Kuifang to win all four ♣ tricks plus the ♠-A for all five and a total of twelve, and she could not discard her ♥-J as that would allow Kuifang to go to dummy with the ♠-A and play the winning ♥-8 and Ms Brown would then be squeezed in both her ♣ and ♦ suits, resulting in a total of twelve. So she slammed her ♥-J on the table, loud enough for the director to look over from the other side of the room, and her partner to look up from his apparent glee in seeing his partner getting caught in a repeating, progressive squeeze, which he had helped set up with his pre-emptive 3♠ bid. At least he took a trick, he would say to her later.

After Bobbi Brown left the table, Kuifang smiled at Ge and said, I think that was a progressive squeeze. I've never had a progressive squeeze in all my years of playing this game; I've never even seen it.

Ge just sat back and admired the beautiful solution—even though it'll be years before he'll find out how to replicate it when the opportunity came up—and the even tempo of its execution, thinking to himself, I'll have to give her a progressive squeeze going down on the express elevator and straining hard to remember if he was actually here playing a game of bridge and not at the American Club on Fuzhou seventy years ago watching his partner and wife execute a progressive squeeze against the opponent with the brushed scarlet passion lip gloss last seen on her way to a matinee showing of *Gone with the Wind* at the Grand, and straining harder yet to find a metaphor to use for a progressive squeeze for his notebook, finally concluding that metaphors are really se-nile detours used by people to rise above the tedium and toil of their lives.

34

Ge did not understand what they were saying, but he could hear and count the syllables and even see the space between them, talking just like the uniformed Imperial Japanese Army or Navy officers he would sometimes see hanging about at the edge of the International District, as if they were barking terse cuss words or marching orders, quite unlike the fake Mandarin rolling around their curled tongues in the Bund's upscale foreign restaurants when they were out of uniform.

But this was not one of them, just a Brauhaus on Hankou Lu around his office famous for its black beer and pork knuckles. Ge was having a beer with his friend Mr. Bogotá *Páshǒu*, and the tables next to them were filled with loud and fat German men ordering black beer carried to the table in tall steins lined up in a row on a narrow, long plank as fast as the short waiter in shorter lederhosen could bring them.

See that man with the foam on his toothbrush moustache, Bogotá Man asked, he lost big last week, ten Franklins in less than thirty minutes, playing All-In on almost every hand. Didn't seem to care at all throwing his money around—must be loaded.

Who was the big winner?

It was that German naval attaché, a *Korvettenkapitän* from the consulate. Funny thing is, he was singing *Ich liebe Mozart* to the tune of *Frère Jacques* every time he had a good hand. Some of us caught this tell right away, but not his countryman who kept on pulling out an endless supply of ten dollar bills from every pocket in his jacket, pants and shirt. An obvious mark, if I might be allowed to use that word.

Of course, of course, Ge answered and waved at the short waiter for two more light Krombachers. So then, you've decided to be a professional card player, he finally asked. These private games with a heavy buy-in?

Bogotá Man looked at Ge cautiously this time. You're not doing a piece on me are you?

No, Ge assured him, I don't even have my notebook with me.

This is the way I see it. China has produced a number of great generals, philosophers and poets who've been bored to death by the lies of the courtesan and academic historians, and so they spend their lives trying to see the other side of the moon, or drown in the lake trying to get there. I, well I, and Bogotá Man raised his glass of beer, I know I can't get there, so I just stay here and look at the prints beneath my shoes instead. It does give me a lot of time to read during the day, he explained.

Ge started laughing easily, soon joined by Bogotá Man at his own joke, the two of them getting louder and louder until they could not hear the Germans any more.

But their memory could still hear the voices of the street hawkers outside yelling *Lucky Strikes. Jack Daniels. Girls. Dovedown nylons. More girls. Hersheys. Whisky. Johnnie Walker. Whisky. Everything. You looking for something we got* and were reminded that the goons of the Dai Li secret service were still compromising everyone's life, and the nine-year old War of Infinite Resistance against the despotic Japanese was still going on and most likely to get a lot worse.

After their laughter settled down, Ge got serious and agreed with Bogotá Man about the cant and lies of the collaborators, public historians, journalists and politicians. Their histories and their memoirs are all here on the bookcases in our libraries. Sometimes when one of these books is opened, he continued, opening the fingers of his right hand, nothing can be heard, only a few spilled words moving a little. Such willful blindness and conscious disregard for the discrepancy between their words and reality. Maybe one day the language will be rectified, making the word match reality.

You want to come to watch the poker game tonight, Bogotá Man finally found a way to get Ge down from his abstract discussion with himself. It'll be at some Dutch Shell's executive's house in the French Concession. Two good players, a couple of American whales, from Oklahoma and Texas, I was told.

I don't know, I've met these Americans before. I don't know about spending the rest of the night listening to these Americans and their insistence that politics should be kept separate from sports, all the while repeating a con about their national sport, football and dissing the black salute at the 68 Olympics in Mexico City and the American women's sign at the Venice Cup here two years ago—you know, you were there at the awards dinner. But sure. Maybe I can concentrate on watching the game and not let their pomp disturb me.

It'll probably just start off innocently with some five card game, stud or draw, but the American oil money will want to switch to their new favorite, Texas Hold'em with a pricey ten thousand buy-in.

As they were leaving the Brauhaus near midnight, Mr. Bogotá *Páshŏu* reminded Ge, When we speak again, perhaps it'll be in the distant past and Kuifang has just sent me the invitation to your wedding.

35

Bobby Fischer was never just about Bobby Fischer, Bogotá Man shook his head and looked across the table at Ge.

He had been right about last week's poker game at the expansive, guarded, three-story house inside an off street compound in the French Concession, its walls spiked with glass and barbed wire. With short refreshment and rest breaks, the game went on almost until the next sunset. The two American whales were from Oklahoma and Texas, and proud of their hometowns of Tulsa and Midland, and kept their Dallas Cowboys hats on during the entire game. After an impatient first hour of stud poker they insisted on changing it to Texas Hold'em with a twenty thousand buy in, more than Bogotá Man had predicted, and called on the French dealer to use a new deck of World Bridge Federation certified and sealed cards from the house safe every thirty minutes.

Ge was also right. At first these Americans boasted that their football was the greatest sport ever invented, and thought it was about time the

International Olympic Committee accepted it as an official Olympics event, especially when they have a friend who's its current president.

Lookit here, the man from Midland said, throwing, running, catching and hitting, hitting, and hitting hard, all the basic physical skills no less, you all see, punching the air for emphasis with the hand not holding his two hole cards. What more is there?

And oh yeah, the women get involved too you see, he added, all those cheerleaders and pom-pom gals on Friday nights.

His friend tilted his Cowboys hat and looked over his cards and across the green felt at Bogotá Man and said for his benefit, You hear now, there're some Chinee high schools down south already playing football in an organized league, don't you know?

This continued into the first refreshment break, the Texas whale buttoning Bogotá Man and Ge at the bar about how the great Cowboys quarterback Roger Staubach was also a great patriot who'd served his country as a naval officer in Vietnam, and continued non-stop when they went back to the table, You know, we also have that colored feller, the World's Fastest Human Being, double gold medalist sprinter in the Tokyo Olympics, Mr. Bullet Bob Hayes. He's not like those two other sprinters in the Mexico City Olympics four years later, traitors to their country with their nigger Black Panther salute and all you know. Hayes, a credit to his race. A credit. Ring of Honor. Hall of Fame I swear.

You're right, Bogotá Man said to Ge out in the street when the lengthy game finally ended late next afternoon, with the Americans successfully appealing to be allowed first a second and then a third buy-in. He had won some, but not as much as the two players from Germany and Italy he suspected were playing as a team, but he wasn't quite sure.

Those Americans and their Texas Hold'em poker. It's nothing but just huff and bluff, a perfect game for them. No skill required, except lying, so American.

Intrigued by the Texan's comment about organized American football in the south, Bogotá Man went back to his apartment after the game to use his computer with his new PandaPow VPN software to check out the rumor on the Internet.

You know Ge, he said next week when they were exchanging notes at the Brauhaus, that man was right. Down in Guangzhou there's a high school league, couple of them coached by retired or injured American professional players. They even have mascot names, like their American counterparts. The leading two teams are the Guangzhou South Tigers and the Guangzhou Goats.

Ge had gone further. I contacted my friend at the Xinhua, and he said there's a plan to begin a ten-team American football league across the whole country. Two teams have already started practicing, the Beijing Guardians and here, here in Shanghai, the Shanghai Nighthawks.

But something's wrong here. The names you know? The guy from Midland emphasized hitting, hitting and hitting hard. Except for the Tigers maybe, the Goats and the Guardians and the Nighthawks don't sound as if they're going to be hitting very hard.

And I also started looking into politics and sports, Bogotá Man added and ordered another beer from the short waiter. Maybe I should say patriotism and sports, no?

That's a most dangerous word, Mr. Bogotá *Páshŏu*, *patriotism*, almost like the word *symbol*. When I took a poetry course at Fudan years ago, the professor forbade us to use that word in his class. "Say what you mean, say what you mean," he repeated the first day of class, and threatened dismissal if we were caught using that word within his hearing.

That's why this subject is so intriguing, Bogotá Man continued. We all know what the Führer wanted to do with his 1936 Berlin Olympics, but the American's convoluted and tormented equation between patriotism or politics and sports is much more telling about its national character than anything else, considering how sports is the most important cultural activity in its daily calendar. We all know how the four gold medalist American black sprinter and jumper Jesse Owens ruined Hitler's attempt to showcase his Aryan racial supremacy with its new 100,000-seat stadium and all the fancy technology for timing, measuring and broadcasting the events, and the Führer's refusal to shake his hand because at least according to his architect Albert Speer, he was annoyed at the colored American runner.

And games too, Ge interrupted, not just sports. Patriotism and games. Look at chess and the American, well, the former American then, Bobby Fischer. Probably the best chess player who ever lived. Definitely the most temperamental. How the entire country cheered him for defeating the defending World Champion, the Russian Boris Spassky in what was billed the Match of the Century that took almost two months to play in Reykjavik, Iceland in the summer of 1972. In the middle of the Cold War. President Richard Nixon sent him a couple of letters congratulating Fischer on his way to the World Championship. Look, I have printed out a copy for you, here.

I wanted to add my personal congratulations to the many you have already received. Your string of nineteen consecutive victories in world-class competition is unprecedented, and you have every reason to take great satisfaction in your superb achievement. As you prepare to meet the winner of the Petrosian-Korchnoi matches, you may be certain that your fellow citizens will be cheering you on. Good luck!

Your victory at Buenos Aires brings you one step closer to that world title you so richly deserve, and I want you to know that together with thousands of chess players across America, I will be rooting for you when you meet Boris Spassky next year.

And you know the irony in all of this, Ge added, thirty years after his championship match Fischer renounced his American citizenship and became an Icelandian.

Well, I found out their friend the president of the IOC was the American Avery Brundage who had voted against the American boycott of Hitler's 1936 Olympics, Mr. Bogotá continued his reporting of American patriotism and sports. After Tommie Smith and John Carlos were on the podium for their gold and silver medals for winning the 200, with their heads bowed and a black gloved hand in salute at the 1968 Mexico City Olympics during the playing of the American national anthem *The Star-Spangled Banner*, Brundage expelled the two of them from Mexico. It was the first and only time an American track-and-field team was not invited to the White House. Some say to this day it was the strongest team the Americans had ever sent to the Olympics. So, Bobby Fischer was never just about Bobby Fischer.

And then there's their football, Ge interrupted. That guy from Midland didn't seem to pay much attention to the physical and cultural impact of such an aggressive and violent sport that promotes hard hitting resulting in permanent injuries accumulated from repeating head concussions, and from this distance of seven thousand miles, we can see the close correlation between domestic violence and football, something their police and doctors and social workers have had to work with on football weekends, especially the men watching the game on their television sets and acting out its psychodrama in the privacy of their homes.

But, Bogotá Man interrupted this time, but, he said, you'll be accused that from this distance you can't know anything about their football, or their culture, or what they do in the privacy of their homes. They'll say all you're interested in is how to steal their toaster technology and sell it back to them cheaper in their six-thousand Walmart stores.

And another thing, Ge added, pretty clear at this point he's had too many beers, some have said football is really a southern game. Check out the traditional big college teams. Every year most of the top ones are from the South, count them—Oklahoma, Oklahoma State, Texas, Texas A&M, Auburn, Louisiana State, Baylor, Mississippi, Alabama, on and on. The game's impact on the national culture, at least the male culture, it's almost as if the South had won the Civil War and now occupies everyone's living room East and West, North and South, and has taken over their star-spangled red-white-and-blue identity that's made in Shenzhen, China, and glued to every Riddell or Schutt football helmet high school, college or pro cradled in the player's arm during the pre-game singing of their national anthem with a military color guard lowering every flag be it state, MIA-POW or corporate, except for the national stars and stripes.

Are you done?

No, not yet, I haven't even started talking about the Venice Cup that's going to be played here at the International Convention Center on Binjiang on the other side of the river, you can see from here, Ge said and pointed in the wrong direction.

36

In an idle moment at the office, Ge opened his files and looked up his review of Sonny Ling's piano recital twenty years back in Beijing's political spring of 1989. That piece had always troubled him even when he was filing it back in Shanghai the next day to meet the pressing deadline of the Friday arts and entertainment section. He remembered thinking at the time that serious writers used language to divulge, interpret and explode, but he ended up writing an innocuous—no, moronic is more like it—piece on Beijing's college-educated women driven to reading Chick Lit because their literary studies were modeled on the pretentious and failed American curricular template which originated in their Ivy League schools. He had missed out on what was really happening in Beijing at the time, not just the relocated official ceremony welcoming Soviet President Gorbachev's historic state visit to China to the airport because T^2 was occupied by the students, but the protest itself, the issues that had led to the three months long occupation of the square, how the government responded to them, and how it was finally resolved.

He was determined at this point to try to recover the opportunity and write something about it. Better late than never, he told himself, fiction or non-fiction, it didn't matter, and started jotting down notes for it, in his notebook, on credit card receipts, on the backs of restaurant place mats, menus and napkins, they accumulated, until he thought Fuck this, I'm just going to write it and see what happens.

Shun Min was assigned the news anchoring position right after graduation from the national broadcasting institute. At three hours a day, ten days a month, no writing or editing or reporting stories, just show up in time for makeup before noon and before six to read the news, it was easy enough, the envy of his classmates who were given jobs as video librarian, station timekeeper and boom operator. For the first two years he put all of himself into his work, each story he read, however short and sometimes ambiguous, carried his most sincere and convincing expressions, his voice pulsing with heart-felt humanity, assuring his viewers of the safe passage of another day. *Trust me, trust me* he had said at least five hundred times a year in the privacy of five million homes, *I will not lie to you*, and the people in the capital believed him, even when the lights sometimes reflected off his glasses.

On the streets he was easy to recognize, and citizens would stop him and articulate their trust, sometimes touching a hand or sleeve, and once, in this country where things numinous have been banned since its liberation in 1949, an elderly woman limping on her left side lightly tugged one of his ears, just to make sure he was not divinity itself.

This April when he was reading a brief story on the evening news about the student gathering in front of the palace, a wisp of anxiety appeared in his eyes, and for the few remaining minutes before the camera focused on the international weather map, his voice sounded distracted, then stumbled once on the temperatures between Karachi and Ulan Bator. After the broadcast, the news producer approached him, concerned about his health and diet. The station manager offered a car and driver to take him home. Slightly cautious from all this attention, he said *I'm all right* carefully three times before they believed him, then rode his bicycle home after wiping off his makeup going down in the elevator. In the approaching twilight of another promising spring sunset, Shun wondered about riding downtown to see the students, but not being a reporter, he went home instead, mentally recounting the number of times these students have gathered here in Beijing he had to memorize in middle school history class: 1900, 1911, 1927, 1966, 1976, and now in 1989, six times this century, although he was not sure 1966 should be included.

That evening as he continued reading a book by another novelist preoccupied with the scar on the national conscience left there by the three years of political aberration between

1966 and 1969—a wound so deep that even now a generation later people still refuse to talk about it, as if it had completely vanished, or had not happened at all, which Shun knew was not true—he heard a soft knocking on his apartment door. All evening he had heard the repeated sirens of police and emergency vehicles passing in the streets, and the excited voices of his neighbors who had gone to investigate the rumors, but as a news professional, he knew that such compulsive curiosity could wait until the stories came into the studio in the morning, after they had been gathered, sorted and checked by knowledgeable persons trained and experienced in interpreting these dramatic events. All he would have to do was read them, all there in the past perfect tense.

Shun opened the door, and a tall man in a long coat introduced himself politely, though he did not need to since Shun recognized him as a key member of the central party's policy-making bureau. Over his shoulders, Shun could see the shapes of two other men standing in the shadows, away from the light.

I can only stay a minute, the bureau member said, let's not waste it standing on ceremony. From your broadcast tonight, we were worried about you. He paused, letting his message time to sink in.

Then he asked, Have you been wondering what's happened to the students?

No, I don't think so, Shun answered.

Do you think like your neighbors that some students have disappeared? That the PLA is responsible?

No, I didn't know my neighbors thought that. I didn't even know there were any soldiers down there.

Those are only irresponsible rumors uttered by peasants. You have done a famous job on television, and we want to encourage and help you, and then with both hands he flashed open his long coat.

Its folds were lined with sheets and sheets of stamped official papers. Here, he said, removing a set from the left and handing it to Shun, here, he said, this will help you understand our carefully deliberated position. This is your new definitive dogma on disappearance. But there's no need to read it, it's official, he added. It says that communicators are forbidden to convey stories about disappearances, ever. They're demoralizing; they can panic the people and destabilize the government. Besides, it's not true: it's not scientific; people don't just disappear.

They both stood there a moment thinking about what had just been said. Shun could hear a man outside his apartment thumbing a butane cigarette lighter, *click, click, click* three times before it was lost in the sound of another passing siren, before that too was replaced by a soft but distinct knocking on his door.

I must go now, the bureau member said and shook Shun's hand.

After he left, Shun continued standing in the middle of his apartment until the official papers dropped forgetfully from his hand. He then spent the rest of the night in a living room chair thinking about what the bureau member had said. Was his visit a warning? It definitely was not a routine visit announcing a policy change—that would surely have gone to the station manager or news director. And why me, he thought. I just read the news that's handed to me ten minutes before I go on the air. Did I betray something when I read the student story tonight and fomented trouble? And soldiers? And disappearances? How does one read a story about disappearances, after all? What would be its effect? And who would believe it? Who can authenticate it, he asked himself, until he remembered some stories he had read in a grey-market American newsmagazine one day when he was waiting for someone in a downtown joint venture hotel lobby, some stories about people disappearing in green Ford Falcons in Argentina and others losing themselves in Los Alamos just before Japan surrendered in 1945. But maybe these were not the same things. Maybe, maybe, he repeated to himself until it was beginning to get light outside.

The news director wasn't in his office when Shun went to see him the next morning. All of the drawers of the news archivist's filing cases and desks were opened however, overflowing with papers, as if someone had been interrupted while trying to file them away. Shun picked up a sheet of paper from the many that were scattered on the floor. *Dateline Buenos Aires, August 7, 1977. Disappeared today, Pepe, Marianna and Angela Mendoza, father, wife and daughter, 27, 23 and infant, witnesses said, whisked away in green Ford Falcon while they were walking along Avenida Florida in broad daylight. No known political activism or membership.* Shun picked up another one, a similar disappearance, Shanghai 1927 and 1937, Nanjing 1937, Warsaw 1939 and 1945, Selma 1966, and on and on, the room full of it, until he got to Hiroshima and Nagasaki 1945.

Dazed, he walked into the lobby and did not see anyone there at all, only gaps where they should have been. As he started out the sliding glass doors of the station building, he noticed too that everything on the outside had entirely disappeared, all of Beijing had absolutely vanished, everything except for his exact double, another Shun Min, walking up the sidewalk to the building as if it too had disappeared. He knew this to be true, he said to himself, because he could tell this story now in the first person, a choice he did not have yesterday. And with that choice, he added a cadenza to his own story:

When there was enough to fill all the ballots in the room, Arias embraced the particulars and stood up. Believe me, it all happened so very fast no one knew for sure it wasn't an act of the imagination. Count them, he said, count them to be sure this isn't something we'd find in tomorrow's papers. It was just as he had said, each piece of paper embossed with all their signatures of secrecy. There was not a single dissension.

In a special edition the next morning, the opposition printed the story anyway, and it included specific names, dates and places for the most part as accurately as we had gathered. Arias called just before the story came on the radio and television.

We have been betrayed, we all promised to be silent, but someone has betrayed us, he said. I tried to tell him it'll be all right, that there was no proof, no corroborating evidence to make them credible, that the republic will not panic. But Arias reminded me we didn't have any evidence either—yet we believed these disappearances have occurred like before, much as we often place our trust in random coincidences and wild repetitions and have in fact come to expect them like children—and then he disappeared entirely, his voice trailing into thin air.

By the time of the emergency council meeting that afternoon, only four of us showed up. We sat at one end of the long conference table trying to reconstruct the details one by one, repeating them again and again, trying to be sure we had not left out anything, anything at all.

Ge read over his story and decided to call it "Definitions." Since it did not contain the word *Tiananmen*, he thought it would pass the scrutiny of both Dai Li's Bureau of Investigation and Statistics and the State Administration of Press, Publications, Radio, Film and Television and Mr. Editor would run it in his own *North China Daily News*, but if he didn't, Ge would send it off to the *Beijing Morning News* that had published his Ah Zee story last year.

37

You look so thoughtful *ma*, Kuifang asked and pulled Ge back onto the sidewalk as he was beginning to cross the street against a red light in front of the Line 2 Lujiazui Metro Station on their way to the International Convention Center.

I was trying to understand, he explained, why the American Transportation Security Administration goons at New York's JFK airport had to destroy Krystian Zimerman's Steinway that travels with him to recitals because they were suspicious of the smell of the glue in his piano.

Kuifang looked at the very serious Ge but could not resist that Maybe they thought he was a terrorist going to blow up Carnegie with his piano.

That doesn't make sense at all, he shrugged and glared at her.

They were on their way to the last day of the quarterfinals of the Venice Cup match between the USA2 and French teams and watching the games on large lobby VuGraph monitors. Kuifang had suggested

Line 2 Lujiazui Metro Station, PHOTO CREDIT: HuYing

paying special attention to the American partnerships because they were using the same bidding system that Ge and Kuifang were learning to play in competition.

Do you see your friend Mr. Bogotá anywhere *ma*?

No, but he's usually late, sometimes an hour, sometimes a week, sometimes sixty years, it all depends if he's tied up in a game that doesn't have a clock.

On Board 81 in the morning of this second day of the 124-board match, the bidding difference on the same hand was alarmingly competitive, but considering the level of the game, Kuifang mentioned to Ge, it was not surprising.

Ge could not follow much of what was going on in the game, but as the ever-faithful student, he wrote down all of its details in his notebook.

Board 81

Dealer-North

Non-vul

Open room

(D'Ovidio)

♠ 962

♥ K75

♦ 843

♣ KQ62

♠ KJ85   ♠ T

♥ 4   ♥ AT98632

♦ AT952   ♦ K6

♣ 874   ♣ T53

(Willard)

♠ AQ743

♥ QJ

♦ QJ7

♣ AJ9

W	N	E	S
	P	3♥	X
P	3NT	P	P
P			

This is a very interesting sequence, Kuifang commented to Ge as they looked at the giant monitor. The opening preempt of 3♥ by the American player sitting East is automatic, right out of the book, taking up a lot of bidding room from the North-South French pair, especially playing teams. Sylvie Willard as South could maybe bid 3♠, a simple overcall, but playing teams, she was willing to take a risk and doubled with her hand holding seventeen high card points and forcing her partner to bid.

By the way, Kuifang pointed out, both American players are wearing identical buttons on their sweaters. Can you see what's on them, she asked, this time without the rising question mark for once.

I think they are numbers. Let's see, yes, 1, dash, 20, dash, 09. What is that, Ge asked.

After several moments, Kuifang answered, Of course, that's the day their President George W. Bush will step down. How weird.

What? Ge repeated, his mantra for the day, first his confusion over the TSA destroying Zimerman's Steinway, then several questions about some of the bidding sequences, defenses and declarer plays on the monitors, and now this, this what is it, a political button about their president, here at the bridge table in the middle of an international quarterfinal match in the prestigious Venice Cup, or ha ha, would it be more accurate to call it an anti-political button? Dai Li or the State Security or Avery Brundage would surely expel them from Shanghai if not put them and their families and everyone else who has come into contact with them in prison for the rest of their remaining days, if they live past their interrogation.

Okay, okay Ge, we know you think Dai Li's goons saw you jay walk when you crossed the street against the light just now, but you'll have to get your head out of your Helvetica typeface and pay some serious attention to this analysis. We're here to learn, not just be entertained.

Kuifang waited a moment before continuing. So Sylvie Willard in her compelling and loose fitting Pierrot suit makes a takeout double promising four ♠s, a good hand, and asking her partner to bid, and her ever or wildly optimistic partner Catherine D'Ovidio looked at her hand, and not wanting to play in a 4-3 fit in ♠s when its distribution is bound to be unusual given the opening preemptive 3♥ on her left, decided to go for it all with her eight high card points and no five-card suit and pulled out the 3NT bidding card and placed it on the table with ambiguous confidence.

The American's opening lead of ♥-T can be a real killer against 3NT, Kuifang continued. For D'Ovidio then, the good news is that West surely can't have more than one ♥, but the bad news is that West must just as surely have the missing top ♠s behind dummy's ♠-AQ743. So she counts what tricks she has, see Ge *ma*? Four ♣s, 2♥s after the ♥-A is played, one in the ♠-A, for a total of seven tricks, needing two more to make the contract of 3NT, and the only place she can get them would be one ♦ and one ♠.

So she wins the opening lead with the ♥-J in dummy, and then leads a low ♠, West's ♥-J winning, followed by a low ♦ to East's ♦-K, and the ♥-A and another ♥ to dummy's ♥-K, West having to discard two diamonds. D'Ovidio then ran four ♣s, squeezing West in ♠s and ♦ until the American was thrown in in one suit for an endplay in the other for nine tricks and making the 3NT contract.

Quite a nice endplay for D'Ovidio, Kuifang concluded her explication, but in some ways it can be argued that the opening 3♥ bid helped her play the hand, you might say *ma*?

In the Closed Room and shown on another giant Samsung monitor across the lobby, the other halves of the two teams were playing each other with the exact same hands. The American Kerri Sandborn was not so lucky when she decided to overcall with 3♠ over the same preemptive opening of 3♥ on her right. The French defenders won with a ♥ opening lead by West, East winning with her ♥-A, followed by a ♥ ruff by West, A and K of ♦s and a ♦ ruff, and adding insult to injury, winning two more ♠ tricks for a total of seven and down four for the Americans and minus 150. With the French making 3NT with the same cards in the Open Room of plus 400 for a net total of plus 550 or eleven International Match Points, a disastrous hand for the USA2 team.

Very, very unlucky, Kuifang said. On this hand the American South decided to make a conservative overcall while the French player a risky takeout double, and with her partner taking a flying jump into 3NT, they won everything. But mind you, Ge, the French were very, very lucky, and you must forget about this hand and their incredible parachute. Don't you dare use this hand to rationalize some future moronic call, the teacher cautioned.

38

Ge was sitting straight up in a chair in a library of books, as if he was surrounded by the black volumes of closed faces at a secret society meeting, and trying to see his interrogators in the shadows of this room lit by a single, naked light bulb.

In your imaginary interview with Dai Li you asked if he knew Julia Child, one of them finally said when he was finished with his cigarette.

Ge thought there were too many old historians here, and their lips were always moving and asking the wrong questions.

There was a pause, a rustling of paper, as if that man had to look up the prepared script. Are you a collaborator or a corroborator, he finally asked.

We know you don't work for the OSS, Chiang Kaishek or Mao Zedong, so who do you really work for, another voice added from the shadows.

When he was arrested this morning and escorted into a black limousine by two men with earbuds and bulging tunics, Ge had been expecting it for several years. To his surprise, he was not pushed, handcuffed or searched.

Sit down, one of the armed escorts asked. They'll just ask you a few questions and let you go.

Right. That's how it always begins. The friendly cop first before the rough stuff.

But before Ge could say that he only worked for the chief editor of his newspaper and that the two of them seem to disagree every day, another one asked why he used the pen name of Renyuan, and if it was to enhance or mask his journalism career.

No, I use it to mark my fiction from what I write for the paper.

So why do you write fiction when you're paid to write non-fiction, or do you think the two are the same?

One by one the thick tomes were leaving the shelves and getting stamped out through the freedom of information legislation, and Ge sensed he was on borrowed time, and that it was only a matter of time before he was also going to be asked if he knew Julia Child, completing and reversing the ten questions he had asked Dai Li sixty years ago.

And why do you spend so much time on music, when you can use it to improve your pitiful bridge game.

Then from the darkest shadows at the end of the room behind a small desk came a familiar, clear voice, more a snort of a horse, asking Why do you not like *Dream of the Red Chamber*?

Ge knew it was Dai Li, and he better come up with a honest, true answer, especially within the realm of the rumor that the revolutionary Chairman Mao loved the book so much he read it once every year, though Ge never understood why.

It was November when I first started reading it, Ge answered. The mercury was dropping, but the number of characters in the novel was piling up. I stopped at thirty and instead tried to concentrate on the detailed description of the manners and customs, cuisine and costuming, but it was all too much and not enough, and it was getting colder and colder into January, and frankly, Mr. Dai, I couldn't give a fuck about any one in the story of that self-absorbed clan, too many stones to turn over.

It's the Chinese *Gone with the Wind*, he added, and it came out one-hundred-and-fifty years before Margaret Mitchell's version on the other side of the Pacific.

There was silence, and seeing that somehow everyone had disappeared and there was no one else left in the room, Ge got up and went outside to the pale blue of an early morning and looked up to see if he could find those satellites that would triangulate his GPS position to let him know which Shanghai he was inhabiting at that moment.

39

By the time they returned to the Convention Center for the last hands of the finals between USA1 and Germany on the last day of the Venice Cup, it was all over the news, on every one of the multiple Chinese Central Television (CCTV) stations and newspapers, both domestic and foreign, both English and Chinese. Krystian Zimerman had done it again, this Polish pianist in his prime who most critics agree was the greatest pianist of his generation. At his debut recital at the recently opened Walt Disney Frank Gehry designed Concert Hall in downtown Los Angeles, just before his final work, Karol Szymanowski's "Variations on a Polish Folk Theme," Zimerman sat silently at the piano for a moment, almost began to play, but turned to the audience and said in a quiet, controlled but angry voice that he could no longer play in a country whose military wants to control the whole world.

Get your hands off my country, Zimerman was quoted on the Internet to have said, and all the media verified each other's references to the Bush administration's plans to use his Poland as a missile shield to protect the

United States, pressuring foreign countries into participating in its secret prisoner renditioning program, and the illegal imprisonment of prisoners and interrogation techniques used on them by the American intelligence services at the Guantanamo Bay Naval Base in Cuba.

When some of the audience walked out shouting obscenities, he responded, Yes, some people when they hear the word military, they start marching. Then he played the Szymanowski variations with such astonishing velocity that the audience responded with deafening cheers and standing ovations. He did not give an encore

What can I say; what can I say, Ge repeated. You burn the guy's piano, and he's going to get you. Only in America can that happen. Chaos all over the place.

Impressive, impressive, Kuifang joined him and shook her head, but also sad, very sad.

Bogotá Man finally joined them at the very last hand, four days late, not bad, not bad at all.

They're looking at the VuGraph on the monitor on Board #32.

I see you're taking notes of this my friend, Bogotá Man looked at Ge. You're writing an article about this Venice Cup for your paper or what?

No, no, Ge defended himself. Just to remember the details so I can study them later, you know.

Yes, too much work, too much thinking, that's why I don't play it, Bogotá Man laughed. Besides, there's not much money in it, compared to the games I've been playing. And by the way, thanks for the wedding invitation. Next Saturday is it?

Ge acted as if he had not heard it and continued to squint at the cards and bidding sequence on the monitor and dutifully writing down all the details even while he was paying more attention to the political manipulation of games, sports and the arts.

Board 32

Dealer-West

East-West vulnerable

Open Room

(Rosenberg)

♠ 86532
♥ 654
♦ AKQ
♣ T6

(vonArnim)

♠ AK97
♥ AKT98
♦ J
♣ K92

(Auken)

♠ J4
♥ Q2
♦ 8532
♣ AQJ73

(Stansby)

♠ QT
♥ J73
♦ T9764
♣ 854

W	N	E	S
1♥	P	1NT[1]	P
2♣	P	2♠[2]	P
4♦[3]	P	4♥[4]	P
4♠[5]	P	6♣[6]	P
P	P		

1 Forcing
2 Super club fit
3 Control asking 1430 for ♣s
4 One
5 Queen?
6 Yes, but no side King

That was a torturous auction, Kuifang commented. Glad it's finally over. Those Germans and Poles with their fancy systems and gadgets, they sometimes trip over themselves, but not this time, perfect for getting to their minor suit slam of 6♣s, especially in this team game, like those high school girls Katherine Ling and Wu Shiung Chien at the Grand Hotel last month. And it's easily makeable in four different ways for a plus 1,370. Let's see how their partners are doing with the same hand in the Closed Room.

They walked to the other monitor and Ge said, Look, both Debbie Rosenberg and Joanna Stansby are wearing those 1-20-09 buttons, and so are a few other Americans around the floor of playing area.

Also, Kuifang continued Ge's sentence, these American players are busily chatting with their opponents during their breaks, at the table and at the beverage station. They look like very energized, serious and excited conversations. Can't be about the clothes they're wearing. But also very friendly.

W	N	E	S
1♥	P	1NT	P
2♠	P	4♠	P
P	P		

Their partners the Jill Twins, Levin and Meyers in the Closed Room got to a reasonable 4♥ contract with a less complicated bidding sequence and easily making six for a plus 680 score, but a net of minus 690 or minus twelve International Match Points. Fortunately USA1 had such a commanding lead of over one-hundred IMPs going into the last sixteen boards that it was a finite improbability they would not win the Venice Cup.

Soon afterwards the four players and their non-playing captain Gail Greenberg were escorted to the podium at the front of the ballroom for the award ceremony. Zhang Ziyi, the mysterious and inquisitive Cute Cute of the recent *Crouching Tiger, Hidden Dragon*, looking distinguished but naughty at the same time, with her hair in a short crop and sleeked back who had been watching the monitors all afternoon in her traditional Mandarin red dress with high collar and white silk frog-button closures down the front and matching Manolo Blahnik Hangisi satin pumps, joined the crowd as it erupted into cheers and congratulations for the USA1 team and its singing of their *Star-Spangled Banner* that was coming over the public announcement system. At the end of their national anthem, Debbie Rosenberg raised over her head what looked like a sign written with dark, brown lipstick on the back of a dinner menu, WE DID NOT VOTE FOR BUSH, that Ge found out later was made in response to several exiled players from the other nations who had walked on their own from one poor country devastated by war to the middle of another one in this country to ask the Americans to clarify their role in them.

PHOTO CREDIT: Swan Game

His mouth wide open, Bogotá Man marveled at how the Americans can say this and not be imprisoned in solitary confinement for life.

Or completely ignored, Kuifang added, like their writers. I'm not sure which is worse.

She found out the next day that for this public act of defiance, several officials in the World Bridge Federation (WBF) and the American Contract Bridge League (ACBL) with the support of most of their world-ranked men players as well as most of their members, called the players traitors and threatened to punish their seditious act by banning them forever from national and international competition.

Fortunately the players had enough support from the more sensible members of these organizations and sanity prevailed at the ACBL executive meeting in San Francisco next spring when these threats from the other, dark side of the moon were voted down, leaving it open that the USA was still a country in which freedom of speech is not threatened by Dai Li or the State Administration of Press, Publications, Radio, Film and Television, and its people were still allowed to disagree, whether it's over a Reykjavik chess championship or the Olympics or the Venice Cup. The players also received encouragement from Natalie Maines of the Dixie Chicks, and the French national team sent their American opponents a letter of support.

You were doing only what women of the world have always tried to do when opposing the folly of men who have lost their perspective of reality.

40

In his library of books then, Ge was not entirely sure how Mr. Editor would react to the cat coming down the tree based on two bridge hands from the 2007 Venice Cup. He might say there's the perennial problem with writing about the technical side of this game that most of his newspaper's readers would find incomprehensible and simply skip this section and go on to the next. Ge had assumed nobody's going to hang out and look for some hidden meaning behind a bridge parable, allegory or symbol, as impossible as it seems, given the polemical references.

But they want an easy to understand narrative arc, Mr. Editor would end up screaming, not something they would use to wrap unrecyclable garbage.

Then the two of them would get into a more heated argument about the merits of *Dream of the Red Chamber* until Ge saw the headlines of yesterday's front page on his desk:

总局发出《关于广播电视节目和广告中规范使用国家通用语言文字的通知》

Administration issues "Notice on Regulating the Usage of the National Common Language and Script in Radio and Television Programs and Advertising"

This is it then, isn't it, that print and broadcast watchdog PPRFT has done it again, Ge said, quoting verbatim:

Authorities at all levels must tighten up their regulations and crack down on the irregular and inaccurate use of the Chinese language, as its casual use will create cultural and linguistic chaos, especially with minors, and must therefore be resolutely corrected.

How can they do this, to a language that's full of puns and homophones, he added. Look, the first word for President Xi is *dà*, and the first word for the First Lady Peng is *má*; put them together, *dàmá* means marijuana.

And so then, they continued arguing, Ge finally admitting that he did like the dream sequence in Chapter 1 of the book that left no stone unturned, and promising that in his future writing he will avoid metaphors and using language to play with double and triple meanings, and will instead resolutely stick to the economic realism of how to find the best holiday discounts in town and hide your cash from the G-Man in Prada bags.

41

Unknown to the ever watchful eye of his editor and agent, there actually were certain things Ge would not write about, including stories based on the daily racing forms from Hong Kong, Macao or Las Vegas. He won't even think about writing the biography of his Fujian Province grandfather who made his fame and fortune as a pirate in the 19th century working the Black Ditch, as he believes this kind of writing will mean his writing career is over, kaput, out the window, ha ha ha, inhaling laughter that scattered crows and magpies, his fellow jokers and critics.

He also knows he's made some serious errors in his work. In his first book he had attributed the Oroqens' exile as the result from killing a bear when in reality they had killed a wolf, and then perpetuating the common assumption that they were exiled from North America to Asia when recent evidence indicates the opposite in this mythical land bridge with the ONE WAY sign that has been easily manipulated to point in any political direction.

Ge has also acknowledged the error on page 70 of the next and middle book of this trilogy where the two main characters got their names switched when they were looking over the Three Gorges Dam in the Yangtze River, though when he's had enough to drink he would blame this on the sloppy work of the copyeditor.

Then there's the ambiguity about his relationship to Kuifang. Are they married, or are they not? There are references to their conversations about getting married, but are they, or are they not? And if they are, was it last year, or seventy years ago?

Nevertheless, Ge has tried to be accurate with the details of this narrative, for which the author and his translator will take full, personal responsibility.

And finally, during the war nobody said anything. Now we speak too much.

$$\log(r) \sin\left(\frac{1}{2}\theta\right) = z \cos\left(\frac{1}{2}\theta\right).$$

TYPEFACE KEY

Main narrative	➔	Times New Roman
Interior monologue	➔	Kingthings Trypewriter 2
Author and translator's notes	➔	Century Gothic
Sidebars	➔	Arial Narrow
Chinese words	➔	*Apple Chancery*
Ge's published work	➔	Lucida Grande
Editor's notes	➔	MrsEaves
Chinese ideograms	➔	Adobe Heiti Std 葵芬 Kuífāng
Chinese ideograms	➔	Baoli SC 总局发出 Administration issues
Chinese ideograms	➔	Weibei TC 郭亚力 Guo Yàlì

REVIEWS OF OTHER BOOKS
BY ALEX KUO

"In his impressive body of work spanning 40 years, Alex Kuo consistently pushes the limits of literary genres while defying some of society's most deeply entrenched assumptions. I came upon Mr. Kuo's relatively recently, yet it is easy to see the influence his voice has had not only on writers but also on our collective views of race, culture and politics. In fusing the political and the literary, Mr. Kuo illuminates over and over again the profound power of the art."

—Medical writer PAULINE CHEN

"This fast paced political thriller offers a much needed fresh and multidimensional examination of student unrest on both sides of the Pacific. By switching points-of-view Kuo shows a literary craftsman at work and proves once again that fiction counts."

—Writer and media critic ISHMAEL REED

"Alex Kuo is a mainstay of Chinese American and Asian American writing. He has helped to create this field by producing some of its most important work and by defining the field. His concerns are large and universal—the ecological landscape of the American West, politics, history, and, of course, human emotions. As a citizen of many cultures, he has taken on the responsibility of integrating his prodigious knowledge of many peoples."

—Writer MAXINE HONG KINGSTON

"This is a story about the parallel histories of the Three Gorges Dam in China and the Grand Coulee Dam in the U.S., a meditation on the emergence of truth from improbable fiction, and a literary illustration of playful seriousness. Alex Kuo is one-of-a-kind writer whose works recall the finest moments in Thomas Pynchon, Michael Ondaatje, and Karen Tei Yamashita."

—Scholar and literary critic WEN JIN

"Alex Kuo's brilliant and original *The Man Who Dammed the Yangtze* tells a parallel tale for our time. Global corporations and their politician minions have come rule. Two startled, compassionate mathematicians—one American, the other Chinese— foresee the disasters that compulsive dam-building will trigger. But their compassion, insight, intelligence and calculus seem no match for the magnitude of arrogance, ignorance, ambition, and wrong-headed greed they confront. From their respective home turf, both G and Ge care about the world's children who will inherit a legacy doomed to be viewed as 'engineering error, human error, unexpected shifts.' Think Three-Mile Island, Union Carbide Bhopal, Valdez Exxon Alaska, Hurricane Katrina, BP Gulf Coast Oil Spoil. Alex Kuo's ocean-swimming, epic poem of a novel, co-locates and pinpoints the back-story to future crisis our planet can be spared."

—Writer, actor and musician AL YOUNG

"Alex was my first writing teacher, and 25 years later is still my teacher. His vision is sure and uncompromising. I love this book."

—Writer and basketball player SHERMAN ALEXIE

"I happen to believe that there are a lot of good poets around at present, but a poet like Alex Kuo, who possesses a highly developed moral sense and a bitter honesty, is rare at any time, and especially in this time. We need him."

—Poet CAROLYN KIZER

For other titles available from redbat books, please visit:
www.redbatbooks.com

Also available through Ingram's, Amazon.com,
Barnesandnoble.com, Powells.com and by special order
through your local bookstore.

www.ingramcontent.com/pod-product-compliance
Lightning Source LLC
Chambersburg PA
CBHW080731250626
47170CB00011B/2902